PRAISE FOR SUSAN DUNLAP
AND HER "FEISTILY ATTRACTIVE"*
BERKELEY HOMICIDE COP, JILL SMITH

"This is no story about a shy little female who makes good as a cop. It's about police procedure and California crazies and the poor and helpless. Chock full of clues, it will lead you on a merry chase until the author is ready to reveal the solution in a dandy climax."   —*Ocala Star-Banner*

"DUNLAP HAS A KEEN EYE FOR DETAIL AND SENSE OF PLACE. SHE GETS BETTER WITH EACH BOOK."   —*Library Journal*

"Dunlap has carved out her own territory in the mystery field."   —*Mystery News*

"Susan Dunlap evokes the sensual details of her characters and their environment with singular talent."   —*The Sunday Herald,* Monterey, Calif.

The New York Times Book Review

Books by Susan Dunlap

JILL SMITH MYSTERIES:

Cop Out
Sudden Exposure
Time Expired
Death and Taxes
Diamond in the Buff
A Dinner to Die For
Too Close to the Edge
Not Exactly a Brahmin
As a Favor
Karma

KIERNAN O'SHAUGHNESSY MYSTERIES:

No Immunity
High Fall
Pious Deception
Rogue Wave

VEJAY HASKELL MYSTERIES:

An Equal Opportunity Death
The Bohemian Connection
The Last Annual Slugfest

AS A FAVOR

A MYSTERY BY

Susan Dunlap

A Dell Book

Published by
Dell Publishing
a division of
Bantam Doubleday Dell Publishing Group, Inc.
1540 Broadway
New York, New York 10036

The trademark Dell® is registered in the U.S. Patent and Trademark Office.

ISBN: 0-440-20999-4

Reprinted by arrangement with St. Martin's Press, New York, New York

Printed in the United States of America

Published simultaneously in Canada

October 1991

10 9 8 7 6 5 4
RAD

For Mary and for Millie

Chapter

1

I crouched behind a clump of daisies in Berkeley's People's Park, keeping watch on my fellow beat officer's patrol car across the street. I was in plainclothes—threadbare jeans and an embroidered blouse—and in my hip purse was my automatic, though it would be damned hard to get at if I needed it.

The late afternoon fog had begun to roll in off the Pacific, shading the park. Now, this park consisted of haphazard clusters of bushes and wildflowers in a field of tall grass and weeds. People passed by it without a thought. But in 1969 the struggle for its possession had been a *cause célèbre.*

Then, street people had built slides and jungle gyms, painting them in psychedelic colors. They planted flowers and vegetable gardens, played guitars, sailed frisbees, and smoked pot. They epitomized the anti-establishment sentiments of the times.

When the University of California announced plans to pave the area for parking, they demonstrated. Students, just finished with final exams, joined in. Thirty thousand people marched through the Berkeley streets. Violence came quickly. National Guard troops, the county sheriff, and police from outside the city were called in. They blocked intersections. They enforced curfews. Helicopters flew low over streets and homes. For two weeks the drumming of helicopter blades kept every citizen aware of the crisis. No one was neutral.

But during those angry days, the Berkeley Police calmed animosities on both sides. To residents they were a different breed, better educated, more liberal, as much "Berkeley" as police.

Now, years later, it was still a police force I was pleased to be part of.

I looked past the east end of the field at Seth Howard's patrol car, across the street.

The patrol cars Howard drove had become the targets of a rip-off artist. Half the time Howard left one, he would come back to find something gone—a windshield wiper, a hub-cap, once even his license plate. If a cop in Berkeley had had one car assigned to him, Howard could have let it go, assuming the end would come by attrition. But we didn't operate that way. We took whatever car was available. At this rate Howard would be responsible for the stripping of the entire fleet.

From behind me came a whiff of dust and sweat.

Across the street, hurrying past Howard's car, was a group of students, laughing, all talking at once, seemingly too absorbed in their own conversations to notice the patrol car. I watched. Ripping off a police car was the type of theft that might appeal to kids with free time at the beginning of the semester.

The dust-and-sweat smell was stronger. This park was no longer the domain of carefree "flower children." It was as dangerous as any park in the city.

A foot hit the soft ground three inches from my leg.

"Watch where you're going!" I glared up at the man.

He was well over six feet tall, and layers of clothing, all filthy, hung off him. His glazed eyes moved erratically as if keeping watch for spectres that never materialized.

He was one of the drug casualties who wandered around Telegraph Avenue or slept away afternoons in the park. He could easily have walked into me.

But he didn't. He veered right and kept moving.

In the last dozen years this area—the four blocks of Telegraph that ran north from Dwight Way to the University campus—hadn't changed much. There were more boutique-y shops, more fake wood and ferns, and the street vendors who had once been local craftsmen were now predominately professionals. Students sauntered along the wide sidewalks glancing at jewelery and T-shirts, and street people still hung around, passing time, staring vacantly, and asking for spare change.

I watched the man amble west across the field toward Telegraph, his hair matted, his jeans discolored and incompletely patched; he was in no hurry; in his life there was nothing that wouldn't wait.

I turned back to Howard's car—just in time. A curly-headed figure yanked Howard's antenna off and ran.

I dashed after him toward the street. A truck passed, blocking my view. When I spotted the figure again, he was half a block away, racing across Durant, headed to Telegraph Avenue where he could run inside a shop or melt into a crowd.

"Stop!" I yelled. "Police!"

He paused momentarily, then kept going. Shoppers leaped out of his way. I chased after, the gun-heavy hip purse banging against my pelvic bone. I crossed the street just in time to see him turn onto Telegraph.

When I reached the corner he was gone. The only movements came from sidewalk vendors closing up their stands, a few dawdlers eyeing the wares for the last time, and groups of sallow street people clustered by bare stucco shop walls. The suspect could be anywhere. In the fading light I hadn't been able to make out his face. I'd only seen him run. I wouldn't recognize his walk. His clothes were baggy. I couldn't even be sure he was a man.

Slowly I started down the street, looking intently at each individual, hoping to make one nervous.

I was within fifteen yards of him when he made his break, running frantically to the corner, across the intersection, and into a fleabag hotel fifty yards off Telegraph.

Pushing aside pedestrians, I ran for the corner and started across the street.

A motorcycle shot through the intersection. I jumped back with only a second to spare. "Watch it!" I yelled, but my words were lost under the roar of the motor.

Panting, I ran through the traffic, past a five-story brick apartment building, and up the rickety steps of the stucco hotel that was just a bit smaller and a hundred times more rundown. It had always been a hotel and it had always been squalid. I pulled the door open and looked into the small lobby on the right. It was empty. Directly ahead was a staircase and a hallway bare but for the doors to the three first-floor studios. There hadn't been time for the suspect to make it up the stairs, but the back door banged against the porch rail. Running to it, I looked out.

The yard was tiny—hard clay ground surrounded by a wooden fence that had fallen years ago. The suspect could have doubled back through the apartment house next door, gone straight along the alley behind the Telegraph shops, or cut left into the giant parking structure to the south of the hotel. In the heavy shadows of dusk there was no sign of him.

Catching my breath, I walked back to the lobby. The high wooden counter with the mail slots behind it was the only indication that the room was a lobby. There was no one behind the desk, no mail in the slots, no bell that would bring a desk clerk running. There might once have been chairs, but if so they had been ripped off years ago. Only a table remained.

I stood a moment, assessing the hall. The clatter of two people running down it had drawn no interest from the tenants. None of the doors had opened.

I knocked on the first of the two doors on the south

side of the hall. No answer. Likewise the one behind it. But from the room behind the lobby a man with stringy gray hair to his shoulders answered. He wore a cheap and none-too-clean shirt and pants that hung loose from his body. His room reeked of wine.

He squinted at me, the folds of his face pulling together to create a surprisingly sharp show of suspicion.

I pulled out my shield. "I'm Officer Smith, Berkeley Po—"

"What do you want, pounding on my door? Can't a man have peace in his own room without city cops and welfare cops banging and snooping? Harassing. It's harassing." His face throbbed red.

"Calm down. I just want to know if someone ran through here a couple minutes ago."

"What?"

I repeated the statement.

"What're you chasing them for?" His face was returning to its normal color; only the broken blood vessels in his nose and cheeks remained red. I'd seen him on the Avenue—drinking coffee at the Mediterraneum Caffe, or talking with groups of people, arms waving, face reddened. He was a regular on Telegraph, one who would make it his business to recognize cops and one who, despite the years of evidence to the contrary in Berkeley, would assume every cop was out to get him.

But there was no point in recounting the department's record. Instead, I geared myself to his reasoning. I said. "You've seen me here on beat, haven't you?"

He thought, then nodded.

"You haven't heard anything about me going after people for no reason, have you?"

"No, but . . ."

"If I *had,* you would have heard. It would have been all over the Avenue."

"Yeah. Okay. Yeah, someone did run through here. And out. I heard the footsteps going down the stairs."

"You sure?"

"Sure as I can be with the racket going on in here. I

didn't go out and look, if that's what you're asking. In this building running down the hall is no big thing."

Taking down his name—Quentin Delehanty—I asked him to call if he learned anything about the suspect.

From the perfunctory nod as he shut the door, I knew he wouldn't.

"Damn," I muttered as I stomped down the stairs. There was nothing to do now but bottle up my frustrations and walk on up Telegraph to the University and wait for Howard.

According to our plan, while I'd watched his car, Howard was to have been making himself visible several blocks away. After an hour—about now—he'd pick up the car and then drive over to get me at the intersection of Telegraph and Bancroft, by Sproul Plaza.

The air had grown chilly; the sweat on my back and face turned cold. Students hurried from campus onto the Avenue. Traffic whished down Bancroft. It was October, and at five o'clock the bay fog had rolled in. As each pedestrian rounded the corner I checked him, but I knew it was hopeless.

When the patrol car stopped, I got in and slammed the door. The radio sounded muffled—because, of course, the antenna was gone.

"You look like you're ready for the Olympic Sweating Team," Howard said as he pulled into traffic.

I could imagine. Any make-up I'd started out with would be gone. My eyes, which varied from green to gray, would be definitely gray by now, and my skin would look like the oatmeal left to harden in the bottom of the bowl. "All in all, it seems fitting."

"So it's thief Six, cops Zero, huh, Jill?"

"I chased him into a fleabag hotel and lost him. He's probably there laughing his insides out."

"How can he keep slipping away? Damn! I've spent more time on this dumb, laughable—"

"I got distracted, Howard. This spaced-out guy in the park almost walked into me. I took my eyes off the car. When I looked back, there he was—the thief. It couldn't

have been more than a minute, the only minute in nearly
an hour when I wasn't staring right at the car." I sighed,
slumping back against the seat. "How *does* he do it?"

"Listen, Jill, I know you did all you could. You couldn't
let yourself be trampled."

I looked over in time to see his grin before it faded
back into the tense lines of his face. His red hair curled
out below his hat and his long legs were spread apart to
avoid the dashboard, even though the seat was all the
way back. There was something very appealing about
those long muscular legs, something I always brushed
quickly from my mind. Howard was a friend, a close
friend; I wanted him to remain just that.

"*You* can force a smile," I said, "but Lieutenant Davis
won't be laughing. Soon he'll have to account for all
those aerials and hubcaps. And you know what he'll do."

"Right. He'll decide the easiest thing is to put me on
foot patrol where all they can steal is my night stick."
The tires screeched as he turned the car left. "Goddamn
it. Before this I had a good record. Now my very presence causes crime."

Howard had every right to be frustrated and to be worried. At any other time he might have waited out the
thief, with the assurance that any appearance of floun-
dering on this case would have been more than offset by
his competent handling of major crimes. But now every
officer needed to look his best. The department was reor-
ganizing. A patrol officer would no longer handle all
cases on his beat, whether they were drug dealing or jay-
walking, shoplifting or homicide. Now murders would
go to Homicide, pandering to Sex Crimes. And beat officers would be left with whatever assignments the detec-
tives in those departments gave them. And with traffic.

As new departments were created and old ones ex-
panded, some patrol officers would be promoted to
detective—patrol officers with good records, who'd
shown they could handle themselves on the street. Howard and I had both dealt with murders. That looked
good. Penny-ante theft—unsolved—did not.

The car screeched to a halt at a red light. "Goddamn it," Howard said, "one Telegraph Avenue psycho is not going to ruin my career. I'm going to get him. I have to explain this fiasco to the lieutenant. But I've got a plan, one with no loopholes. You with me, Jill?"

"Sure."

Chapter

2

The University sits in the center of Berkeley where the eastern hills meet the flatlands. The city was created around it. University Avenue runs west to the freeway and the Bay.

From the Berkeley hills west, wealth decreases with the elevation. Houses that start at more than six figures hang precariously off the hillside. Every few years the winter rains pound, the land slips, foundations give way, eucalyptus trees topple onto roofs. In autumn after six rainless months, dry grass catches fire, and homeowners spray their roofs hourly—and hope. The spectre of the Big Quake is always there.

The half mile between College Avenue and Telegraph is flat, and filled with large older homes, some, like Howard's, shared uneasily by four to six acquaintances, some converted to student apartments.

Half a mile further west, Howard turned off University south on Grove and made a quick right into the station lot. By now he wasn't talking. I didn't need to ask why. Explaining the loss of a suspect to Lt. Davis was a daunting prospect.

We walked silently up the side steps to the second floor. Howard knocked on the glass door of the cubicle to the left—Lt. Davis'—and I kept walking past the meeting room into the squad room.

Now, just after six, it was virtually deserted. Twenty wooden desks in three rows filled the room. At the beginning of our shift—Day Watch, 3:00 to 11:00—beat officers headed for their desks and frequently found them still held by their Morning Watch occupants. Everyone was anxious to pass on tips, discuss suspicious behavior on their beats, to ask for follow-up assist. The squad room had the atmosphere of a bus station. But now it was almost empty. I walked halfway down the aisle to my chair, glancing briefly at the front desk to my right. Nothing going on there.

I slumped into the chair. The room matched my spirits. At the sunniest of times the small high windows on the east side were too far away to allow much light to reach my desk. Now the fluorescent lights made the windows darker.

Checking my IN box, I skimmed and discarded a memo reminding us not to park personal cars in the station yard, filed two lab reports, and fingered a message from Nat. Nat, my ex-husband.

"What does he want now?" I muttered aloud.

I looked toward the lieutenant's office, hoping to see Howard emerge, ready to discuss the case. But there was no movement through the doorway.

I glanced back at the note, feeling the familiar pulls of anger and guilt.

At the reception desk, twenty feet away, a woman placed a bundle of clothing in front of Sabec, the desk man. A boy about ten looked scared.

"Tell the officer how you found the clothes," the woman said.

The boy hesitated, undoubtedly wavering between fear of the uniform and elation at his own importance. Fi-

nally he said, "Me and Joey, my friend, we were down by
the Bay and Ralph, my dog, he—"

"They're good quality," the woman interrupted. "The
dress is linen; it's monogrammed, see—AMS—so it was
ordered, if not handmade. I—"

"Is it blood?"

"Ssh." She pulled the boy's hand away from the dress.
"It's been torn, Officer."

"Yes, ma'am, I see. Now, son, you and your friend
found these clothes . . ."

"Joey, that's my friend, well, he—"

"Ready?" It was Howard, looking not unlike the pile of
garments on Sabec's desk—definitely limp, and figura-
tively bloodstained. I opened my mouth, but before I
could form the question, Howard said, "Let's go. I'll tell
you about it at dinner."

"So what did the lieutenant say?"

We were seated in our regular booth in the back of
Priester's on Telegraph Avenue.

Howard forked his lettuce, then paused. "The lieutenant commented in detail, in minute detail, about our losing the suspect."

"You mean *my* losing the suspect."

"That's not how the lieutenant sees it. You, at least,
were within a few yards of the suspect. I wasn't even
within a block."

"Well, that's how we planned it. You were supposed to
be *seen* away from the car."

It was an understatement. A six-foot-six redhead, Howard never went unnoticed. In newspaper stories on the
Berkeley Police, he was always pictured. Twice, a shot of
Howard towering over his patrol car had accompanied
stories with which he had no connection at all. Howard,
the archetypal cop.

Even now as I glanced at the booth across from us, a
blond, curly-haired young woman was staring at Howard. "I see your point," I said to him. "You seem to have
attracted a Little Miss Muffet."

He looked over and sighed. "Wonderful."

I finished my burger. "Did the lieutenant say anything else?" Howard's burger lay barely touched.

"Oh, yeah. He said, one more day. Then, no thief, no car. And definitely no hope of making detective."

I put my hand on his arm and gave it a squeeze. "We'll get your thief. Come on, have a little confidence in us. And in the meantime, eat some of that mound of food you ordered."

A trace of his normal grin returned. "I take it that means you'll help with my ultimate plan?"

"Sure. Tell me."

"In a minute. I'm taking your advice and eating now." Eyeing my empty plate, he added, "There's nothing holding you back from talking. Tell me what you have on for the rest of Watch."

I sat back, fingering my coffee cup. "Not much. A couple of routine follow-ups that I could put off. Some reports. Oh, and a message to call Nat."

Howard took another bite of his burger. He was one of the friends who had heard all my complaints throughout the divorce. The couple of times he had met Nat it was obvious they disliked each other. Whether the cause was merely natural antipathy or because Howard was my friend, I had chosen not to consider.

Now Howard asked, "What did you ever see in Nat? Take your time. I've still got salad and dessert to eat."

I leaned back against the booth. "It's something I've asked myself. Probably the answer is excitement and a certain amount of snobbishness. Nat's family was so wonderfully patrician, so almost Boston-Brahmin. And then, Nat and I were going to Europe, going to live like the literati in the twenties. And he was going to be a professor, which to a college senior like me was virtually next to God. He knew exactly what he wanted and it sounded fine to me."

Howard started in on his salad.

It was the job that had changed me, that and growing four years older. We'd moved to Berkeley when Nat started graduate school and I'd taken the Patrol Officer's test hoping for a job to support us during that time. Our stay in Berkeley was to be temporary, a necessary period until Nat graduated and our real life began.

But I had come to love Berkeley, with its warm winters and dry summers, its street artists, the coffee houses, the campus haranguers, the Telegraph Avenue freaks, and the atmosphere that gave them freedom. I enjoyed the pottery studio that was open till midnight, where on my nights off I could throw lopsided bowls and call them artistic. I liked my friend Sarah, who worked part-time and shared a tiny house because she wasn't willing to sell any more of her time, and Lydia, who designed and sewed wild and wildy expensive vests and dresses, and Jake at Super Copies, the poet—all the people who would never become staid and grown up. I wasn't willing to leave Berkeley, or my friends, or my career.

"Besides my own feelings, Howard, it became evident that I was not likely to be an asset as the wife of an aspiring professor."

"How so?"

"Look how I spend my time. I chase suspects down alleys no sensible woman would walk in. I deal with overdoses and assaults. I break the worst possible news to wives and parents. Frankly, after all that, Nat's concern with the Yeatsian interpretation of life often seems a bit trivial to me. And, I must admit, our divergence has not been one-sided. Nat accused me of an unnatural fascination with the squalid."

Howard laughed.

"The thing is that instead of divorce being the end to a marriage, our marriage was more like a preparation for the divorce. Once I realized I didn't want Nat's life there was nothing else there. In the end it was more a matter of removing my possessions than myself."

"Oh? What about the hibachi? What about," he paused for effect, "what about the seventeen untouched cans of Pepperidge Farms soups? What about . . . ?"

"Okay, okay. Admittedly we hit new levels of immaturity after the separation." We had squabbled over a coffee grinder neither of us had ever used, and the blender, and the houseplants. It had come to a head in September while I was working on a murder case and Nat was calling me about our Cost Plus stainless. "But I did buy him a new set of stainless, and he is going to split the *National Geographics*."

"And this finishes it?"

"I'd like to think so. I just wish he'd realize that the reason you divorce someone is so you don't have to deal with them."

"You *could* ignore his call."

"I could, but you know I won't." I still felt the guilt, not about our possessions or moving out. But my departure had forced Nat to leave school, to take a job working at the welfare department, which he hated. It wasn't logical for me to feel responsible, but I did. I couldn't explain it to Howard; it wasn't even really clear to me.

Howard ate in silence.

"Anyway," I said, "I'm safe now. We've haggled over everything but the stamps and the straight pins. Maybe Nat wants to give me something he took."

"You know you'll have room for it, whatever it is."

"Hey, no sneering at my apartment."

It was still early for most people's dinner, but Priester's was getting crowded. The blond Miss Muffet had been replaced by a duo in jeans and T-shirts. Out front the noise level rose.

"You can eat and talk," I said. "Tell me about your plan."

"Okay." He chewed the remains of the salad and shifted a slice of cherry pie in front of him. "I'm going to get my thief on my own ground, away from Telegraph, where there are no head shops for him to run into, no street artists to hide him, no spaced-out freaks for him to use as camouflage."

"How?"

"Lure him. I'll cruise down Telegraph twice, then park a couple blocks away and leave the car just long enough for him to salivate. Then I'll snatch it away and park a few blocks further on. By the time I get to College Avenue his tongue will be hanging out and I'll grab it."

"That's a fairly disgusting picture, Howard, but if you don't lose him it could work."

"It should take about an hour for me to make it to College."

"Okay. I'll be there."

Howard grinned. "That'll give you time to call ol' Nat and see what he's decided to give you."

Chapter

3

I tried Nat. He wasn't home. My obligation paid, I tossed the message into the garbage and pulled out my pad. I would have to record this afternoon's fiasco. I wanted to slant the report, to somehow make this, the third attempt to capture this very minor thief, look less inept than it seemed.

My phone buzzed.

"Patrol Officer Smith," I said.

"Jill? It's Nat. You didn't call me back."

"I tried. You weren't there." Already the conversation had that familiar accusatory theme.

"I went to Anne's again. She still wasn't home. You remember my telling you about Anne."

I didn't remember. I could feel my fingers tightening on the receiver. Who was this Anne who had gone out? A girlfriend? And, more to the point, why was Nat calling me, at work, to ponder her whereabouts?

In the background I could hear traffic sounds. "Are you in a phone booth?"

"Yes. I'm a couple blocks from Anne's."

"Uh huh."

"I called you before. Anne's missing. I haven't seen her since yesterday; she didn't come to work, didn't call in. It's not like her. Everyone's worried."

But presumably *everyone* was not worried enough to go to her house or call an ex-wife to talk about it. Now I remembered Anne, Anne Spaulding—she was one of Nat's co-workers at the welfare department. I hadn't met her, but Nat had talked of her—how interested she was in his studies, what clever points she had made. He had hit me at low moments when I first moved into my apartment, when it bothered me that the apartment was merely a converted porch at the back of someone's house, when I felt aimless, when I missed not him but the supposed order of our life together. And when I felt guilty about leaving him. Anne, by his description, was all that I had not been, someone who could be the ideal professor's wife.

"Maybe she forgot to call," I said.

"Anne doesn't forget."

"Well, then something probably came up and she was too rushed to call."

"I doubt it. The morning paper's still on the stoop. I pounded on the door. There was no sound inside."

"Are you sure she heard you? What's the layout of the apartment?"

"I don't know. I've never been inside. But, Jill, Anne was at work yesterday. She wouldn't just wander off on a Tuesday morning and forget all about her job. If it were Monday, maybe, just maybe, it might have been a long weekend, although that's not like Anne. But no one is too preoccupied to come to work on a Tuesday."

I could hear the concern in Nat's voice; it was an undertone I hadn't heard in a long time—in two, three years, maybe. I almost asked him how come he hadn't been in Anne's apartment, after all her interest in him. But I stopped myself. Why should I care? He was obviously upset; I didn't need to poke the wound. It was bad enough he was working at the welfare department in-

stead of in classes he loved; I should be pleased he had
some companionship there.

And Nat's conclusion *was* logical. Normal people did
not disappear on Tuesdays. "Okay," I said slowly. "Did
you see the neighbors?"

"No. They probably hadn't gotten home from work
yet."

"Any signs of forced entry?"

"What do you mean? Broken windows?"

"Well, more subtle things, like jimmied locks or trampled branches under the windows or—"

"Jill, there could have been things I didn't notice. I'm
not an expert." He paused. "Will you go and have a
look?"

"Okay, I'll do that."

"Anne lives—" A truck passed, muffling Nat's words.

"What?"

"She lives on College Avenue. That's your district, isn't
it?"

"You mean my beat? Yes." District was a welfare term.
Already I was sorry I'd agreed to help him. That incor-
rect term, replacing mine with his, was typical of Nat. It
summed everything up.

But regardless of my unsettled feelings toward Nat, or
my history of resentment of Anne Spaulding—or maybe
because of them—I would investigate. Anne Spaulding's
disappearance did sound suspicious. This could be a legitimate Missing Person's report.

"She lives just this side of Claremont," Nat said. "I'll
check the house number."

Another truck passed. The operator demanded another payment. The coins clanged.

Nat came back on the line, reading off the street number. I got out a form and said, "I'm taking this down as a
report."

"Don't do that. Anne might not like it."

"Look, Nat, either she's missing or not. If it's not serious enough for a report, maybe you should wait till tomorrow."

It was a moment before he said, "No. That's too long."

"Okay, have you called her relatives?"

"She doesn't have any. I asked Alec—Alec Effield, our supervisor. Anne came from back East, two or three years ago, and if she had any family they'd be back there. But she certainly never mentioned anyone."

"What about friends, lovers?" It was a legitimate question, one I would have asked in any investigation. Over the phone, though, there was no way to tell whether Nat's silence was due to chagrin at the possibility of lovers or at my bringing it up, or whether he was merely attempting to remember who Anne knew.

"She never mentioned friends. In fact she talked very little about her personal life."

"So what you're saying is that you don't know any more than her address?"

There was another silence that I took for acquiescence.

"Okay," I said. "I'll check, but it's probably no big thing. Most likely she'll be home, exhausted from a rushed day in San Francisco, and annoyed to have to talk to the cops."

Again Nat was silent, and I wondered if he were reconsidering the whole thing.

"Jill?"

"Yes?"

"Will you call me when you get back?"

This *was* important to him. "Sure," I said. "I'll call."

"Thanks. I'll be home by nine." He hung up.

I sat staring at the phone, feeling my resentment mount. Nat was concerned, all right, but not worried enough to interrupt his evening's plans.

I had given Nat special treatment. I hadn't made him come to the station, or wait for an officer to come out. In truth, had he been a stranger, I wouldn't have taken a Missing Person's report from him at all, but told him to find someone closer to Anne to make it.

Be that as it might, I was committed. I still had half an hour before I was to meet Howard. I got the keys for one

of the patrol cars and headed for the parking lot. There I
climbed in, moved the seat forward, called the dispatcher, and pulled into traffic.

It was nearly seven o'clock. The sun was dropping toward the bank of fog that pushed steadily in from the
west. On Shattuck, students wrapped heavy Peruvian
sweaters around the halters or T-shirts that had been ample four hours ago. I headed east crossing the still-
crowded area around Telegraph Avenue. The street vendors who had filled the sidewalks earlier were gone, but
university students still hurried to night classes and the
Avenue regulars still propped themselves along walls
and begged for spare change.

I drove past People's Park, empty now, and turned
south on College.

The building Anne Spaulding lived in was a quarter of
a mile north of the blocks of small shops—butchers,
flower shops, bakeries and fashionable used-furniture
stores—the area most people thought of as College Avenue.

Making a U-turn, I parked in front of Anne's. It was an
apple-green duplex circa 1930. Above the double windows on both floors the stucco was embossed with styl-
ized fruit designs. On the building's twin across the fence
to the south, the fruit had been painted rust and saffron,
the leaves aquamarine, a color scheme echoed by the
doors and window frames. But this building was just ap-
ple green. Even the effect of the lattice windows was
muted by the white lining of the drawn drapes behind
them.

The morning newspaper lay on the stoop. I rang the
bell and waited. There was no answer. I rang again,
scanning the door for signs of forced entry. There were
none.

Starting up the driveway, I checked the windows and
the bushes under them. The foliage was thin and yel-
lowed by the dry summer, but showed no signs of having
been disturbed. Anne Spaulding's flat was four steps up
and the windows were higher than eye level. Curtains

still covered them, on this side, too. Either Anne was
very cautious or she hadn't been home during the day.

There was no garage at the end of the driveway. The
two lanes of cement merely stopped at the property line;
from there a macadam path cut between houses to the
next street. Paths bisecting long blocks were not uncom-
mon in Berkeley, but they normally went all the way
from one street to the next; ending in a driveway was
unusual.

Anne's backyard, to my right, was enclosed by a five-
foot-high wooden fence. I glanced over the top, checking
for occupants, pushed open the gate and made my way
through ankle-deep weeds and ivy to the steps.

The back door stood open.

Chapter

I mounted the steps, calling Anne's name. The kitchen was dark. Dirty dishes from a pile in the sink spilled onto the counter. Ahead there was a light on.

"Anne!" I yelled. Still no reply. I hurried into the living room and stopped.

Nat was right to be worried. A chair lay overturned. The bedroom door was half open. A shattered porcelain lamp lay on the floor before it, its pieces brown, bloodstained. Dried blood marked the wall.

Involuntarily I swallowed, preparing myself for what I might find in the bedroom. Using a tissue to avoid smearing any possible fingerprints, I pushed back the door and walked inside, checking in the closet, the bathroom, and under a pile of bedclothes.

The room was a shambles, but there was no body—no stench of death. At least that was a relief. I made my way back to the living room and called the dispatcher for a back-up unit and the lab crew.

There was nothing to do till they arrived. I stood away from the stains, trying to picture what had happened, and the person it happened to. But as I searched my memory for an impression of Anne Spaulding, I realized that Nat had said very little about her (he had not met her till after we'd separated) and what ideas I did have came more from my reactions at the time than from facts. My best move would be to start from scratch.

I looked around the living room. Drawn curtains blocked the windows, but the ceiling light had been left on. A leather loveseat stood opposite the fireplace; matching Barcelona chairs, one overturned, flanked it, and before it was a glass-on-chrome table partially covering a small oriental rug. By the kitchen an etagere held the stereo, albums, and a nine-inch television, but no books and no plants.

Despite the predominance of brown, it was a cold room, more like a display model than a home.

But the bedroom was just the opposite. This had to be where Anne did her living. Heaps of clothes littered the floor and the unmade bed. The walls were white, the bed and dresser had a Salvation Army look, and a third of the room had been made into a sort of gymnasium with dumbbells, exercycle, bust developer, sunlamp, and pulleys attached to a giant hook. The only decoration was a poster for "Theater on Wheels."

In the closet, stacked with care amidst a pile of lace nightgowns and soiled bikini pants, were two pairs of skis—downhill and cross country—and a Wilson tennis racquet endorsed by Chris Evert.

This was the room of someone who viewed her body as one might a sportscar—a machine that, well maintained, will provide pleasure and excitement.

The doorbell rang.

"Jill," Howard said as I pulled it open, "I was wondering what happened to you. I circled a block half a mile north of here—three times. I was just about to park when the call came through."

"Oh, sorry." Howard's thief had completely vanished from my mind. "I thought this would take twenty minutes maximum, but it looks bad in here."

I nodded to Connie Pereira as she rushed up behind Howard, and I was about to speak when the lab van pulled up and the crew eased out.

"Do the lamp and the door jambs for prints," I said as they walked up the steps. "And get the blood on the wall."

The lab man nodded.

"Take a look at the yard for footprints, if you can find anything through the ivy."

"Right, but there's not much chance. What ivy doesn't prevent, it covers."

I shrugged. "Start with the yard; it's already pretty dark out."

Turning to Howard and Pereira, I explained Nat's request. "As far as I know, Anne Spaulding was at work at the Telegraph office of the welfare department yesterday."

"That would be eight-thirty to five, then?" Pereira asked.

I thought a moment. The eight-hour day in government offices varied a bit throughout the state, some counties working eight to four-thirty, some eight-thirty to five. I nodded; Pereira was right. "I assume she was there all day, but I'll have to ask Nat."

"Do we know what she was doing afterwards?" Howard looked at the upturned chairs.

"That's something else I'll have to ask."

"Presumably," Pereira said, "whatever it was ended up here."

"Right," I said. "Let's see what this place can tell us. Howard, you want to take the yard? The lab man should be through in a couple minutes."

"Okay."

As he headed through the kitchen I could see the fading light from the back windows. Why couldn't Nat have called earlier, when there was still enough light to do a decent job?

"I suppose that leaves the kitchen for me," Pereira said.

"And the living room. If you'd seen the bedroom you'd know I was doing you a favor."

I followed the lab crew into the bedroom, checking through the piles of clothing—clean, washed but unironed, dirty—and the more homogeneous clutter of sweatshirts, sweatpants, shorts, T-shirts, and leotards that had found a home on the closet floor. Despite the overwhelming picture of disorder the room presented, each pile contained a specific variety of garment and the slips and blouses from the "dirty" pile had not invaded the "clean" or the "unironed." While the room did make that suggestion about Anne's character—order within disorder—it told me little more. There were no letters, no notes—only a movie schedule and a Theater on Wheels handbill advertising Ionesco's *Rhinoceros*.

I moved on to the bathroom.

It was a small room, obviously a necessity squeezed uncomfortably into a hallway when the building had been converted into flats. A stall shower occupied nearly half the floor space and a waist-high quilted cabinet stood by the bedroom door. I opened the medicine chest and found it surprisingly neat. Bottles of Vaseline, deodorant, Maximum Tan tanning oil, make-up in beige and alabaster pink, eyedrops, and astringent stood in rows with no space unfilled. Nothing could have been removed.

Turning to the quilted cabinet I squatted and pulled open the door.

Pereira came in, looked and whistled. "She must have been either a real beauty or an utter witch to justify this investment in make-up."

I laughed, and the unnatural sound that came from my own throat made me aware of how tense I was. Pereira continued to survey the bottles and tubes in amazement. For Pereira, the Department's investment maven, this type of extravagance was almost a personal affront. Connie Pereira spent her leisure hours taking classes in accounting, tax law, and commodities strategies. All that kept her from making a killing was a set of parents and two brothers who drained off her savings on a regular basis.

She held up a bottle of Corn-Silk Blonde. "Look at this. So her hair wasn't natural either."

I nodded as she replaced it in the cabinet. "What did you find in the kitchen and living room?"

She shrugged. "Nothing hidden in the living room. And almost everything in the kitchen is out, waiting to be washed. There are some vegetables in the fridge, two place settings of bone china stacked away, clean, and the usual assortment of liquor."

Going to the etagere, I fingered through the varied collection of albums.

Pereira followed. "Jill," she hesitated. "I forgot to tell you that I let the lab crew go. Okay? The print man said they were in a hurry."

It was my case. Technically only I could release them. I said, "Did they finish everything?"

"Oh, yes. You want what they got so far?"

"Uh huh."

"Hendricks took samples of the blood—he's sure it's blood—but you know how long it'll take to get a report from the lab."

I knew indeed—two to three weeks normally; in an emergency, three days or so.

"There were prints, but they couldn't say how clear. They didn't know if any would be whole. And the purse, they checked . . ."

"The purse!"

"Right. It was under the sofa."

Now it sat on the table—leather, slightly used purse, an everyday bag.

"There's the usual stuff—aspirin, make-up, keys, wallet," Pereira said. "No cash, but nothing else seems to have been removed. Her driver's license is here and she must have ten credit cards."

I sighed. "A woman doesn't leave home on her own and not take her wallet." Glancing down at it, I looked at the credit cards, social security card, and a health plan card. Nothing unusual.

"These were in the purse." Pereira indicated three pieces of yellow paper—two scraps and one eight-and-a-half by eleven.

"Did they check them for prints?"

"Yes."

I picked up one of the smaller pieces. It was a list, but the writing was crabbed and slanted to the left, and the words virtually illegible.

I held it out. Pereira stared and after a moment said triumphantly, "Spinach . . . eggs . . . you want me to go on?"

I handed her the second paper. "No. Try this."

She stared harder, a line creasing her smooth forehead. Finally she said, "Er–men–tine. Ermentine Brown 20? What do you think Ermentine Brown 20 means? Age? Size? Amount?"

"Could be anything."

The larger paper, a full-size notebook sheet, had been crumpled, then straightened and folded. Judging from the worn edges, it had been in the purse some days.

Pereira and I surveyed it.

"Theater on Wheels," she said, pointing to the childish printing on the bottom. "It'd be a real challenge to identify the blob above that."

"Take a look at the handbill on the bedside table. It's the final product. What we have here must have been her first, very preliminary sketch for the *Rhinoceros.*"

"My God, that's a rhino!" Pereira rushed into the bedroom and a few moments later returned smiling. "It's certainly a metamorphosis."

"Still, where does all this," I gestured to the overturned chair, the blood, the disordered bedroom, "leave us?"

"Fight. Spur of the moment?" Pereira offered.

"Maybe. A kid turned in some clothes, probably bloodstained, torn. They were monogrammed—'AMS.'"

"Anne M-something Spaulding? Hmm. You think it's a sex crime—I mean from the ripped clothes?"

I leaned forward, tapping on the glass of the coffee table. "I hope this isn't the first of a series, like that psycho last year, you remember, the guy . . ." I stopped, staring at the coffee table. My breath caught.

Lying atop one of the chrome supports was a pewter pen, a pen not engraved but with the simple, elegant lines that typified a gift in Nat's family. This *might* not be the pen Nat's father had given him three years ago, but if it was not, it was its double. And when in two or three weeks, or three days or so, the lab report returned, Nat's fingerprints on the pen would be mentioned. It was the only real clue in the apartment.

I took a deep breath. The only clue pointed to Nat, Nat who had told me he'd never been in this place.

Where exactly had Pereira found it? I opened my mouth to ask her just as a great roar came from the apartment above.

Chapter

5

"What was that?" Pereira demanded.

"Sounded like an avalanche," I said.

The initial roar had abated and a second began. With Pereira, I headed for the stoop and banged on the door to the upstairs flat.

There was no response, just a swelling of noise. I pounded again and got no reply, then tried the door. It had been left unlocked—a practice too common in Berkeley.

As I pushed it open, an explosion of sound forced me back. It smothered all other noises and there was no way to tell whether the room upstairs held one deaf old lady or a score of armed revolutionaries. I motioned Pereira to follow me up a staircase that rose steeply between fuchsia walls. Automatically, my hand poised over my holster.

At the landing, vapors of incense thickened to a gray haze that curtained off the room. Squinting, I made out gaudy posters of Oriental deities along the walls of a room furnished only with floor pillows, a tape recorder, and four speakers. Facing a statue, a lone man sat cross-legged, unmoving.

With Pereira waiting at the landing, I moved up beside the man, stood, and when there was no response, put a hand on his shoulder.

His eyes opened slowly and seemed to glisten against the pale angularity of his face. Even his light brown curly hair seemed to soften. The hair started far back on his forehead, so that his features appeared to have been set low down on his head, rather like a short letter typed on an eleven-inch sheet. But unlike many such faces where eyes, nose, and mouth are tiny and seem to huddle together against the vastness of the skin around them, this man's features were full—his eyes were blue, a royal blue that appeared just freshly painted on; his nose was fleshy with soft bumps below the bridge and at the bottom; and his lips were full. Indeed, his features would have been jammed on a smaller face.

He wore a loose white outfit that appeared overlarge on his slight frame.

"I'm Officer Smith," I yelled, extending my shield through the smoky air.

He glanced at it, and back to me, his face set in an expectant smile.

From either side of the room, the noise crashed over my head, beginning a new triad. "The tape," I shouted. "Could you turn it off?"

It was a moment before he said, "Yes, of course," in an uninflected voice that mimicked the three-part beat of the tape. Dipping his head to the poster before him, he rose and pushed in a button on the tape recorder.

The sudden silence was startling. Traffic noises from College Avenue were inordinately clear. The bright colors of the posters seemed more intense, and even the pungent scent of the incense seemed sharper.

"I'll need your name," I said in a voice that was much too loud.

"Harvey Fallon."

I stared at his guru suit and I could feel a smile creeping onto my face.

He smiled, too. "My students call me Sri Fallon. I try to keep things simple, but it's a bit much to expect a novice to call his spiritual mentor Harvey."

I laughed cautiously, afraid my relief would bubble up in gales of unprofessional hilarity. Turning, I motioned to Pereira, and she headed back downstairs.

Harvey Fallon's face dropped into what appeared to be an unnaturally serious expression. "Have you brought a complaint?"

"No. Were you expecting one?"

"There have been some, other places I've lived. A chanting ashram is not always accepted as a neighbor."

"I can imagine," I said. "But I'm here about Anne Spaulding."

"Who?"

"Your downstairs neighbor."

"Is something the matter?"

"She may be missing. This is just a preliminary investigation." She could be dead, but Harvey Fallon didn't need to know that. Taking out my pad, I asked, "Do you live alone?"

"No one into expanding his consciousness lives alone. But you mean on the material plane, don't you?" Without checking for my response, he continued, "I'm in charge of the ashram. Whichever devotees wish to stay here, do."

"And last night?"

"Only I slept here."

I made a note of that. "And earlier that evening?"

Fallon sank smoothly to the pillow, motioning me to one opposite. I declined.

"I got here about six o'clock," he said. And watching for my reaction, he added, "I'm a teller at the Bank of America."

When I smothered my surprise, he continued. "Some time in the middle of last night's session, around ten o'clock, I had a follower, a man—I don't know his name.

Ours is a very loose organization, if you can call it even
that. People come and go. I keep no records. It's not like
we're tax exempt, or for that matter, that there's anything to tax."

"About the man?"

"He was very upset. He kept moving around, fidgeting.
He was nowhere near calm enough even to follow the
chant."

"And?"

"After a few minutes he left. That's unusual. Most
times the chant is so powerful that it overwhelms any
problem."

"Mr. Fallon, what happened after this man left?"

"Nothing. It was only his reaction that was strange. He
hadn't been gone too long when the Kirtan ended."

"Kirtan?"

"Chanting, like the tape of the Tibetan monks you
heard."

"That was chanting!" I said before I could stop myself.
It had sounded more like a herd of sea lions.

Fallon's mouth slid into a smile that showed no trace
of censure, but his tone was serious as he said, "Tantric
chants—Cho-ga. The chants, the incense, the decor—it's
all aimed at overwhelming the senses. Our goal is to
overload the circuits of our sensual responses and be left
with only the interior awareness. The chant is very powerful. You get caught up in it, you become it, it becomes
you." He paused, looked directly at me and said, "Perhaps you would enjoy coming? Any time."

"Thank you," I said, sitting down on a pillow. The air
was clearer down here.

Glancing around the room, I could easily see how Fallon created his effect. Every foot of wall and floor clam-
ored for attention: pictures fighting candles fighting stat-
ues, incense burners and brass bells. On the floor one
pillow was brighter, busier, more intricately designed
than the next.

Focusing with relief on Fallon's simple white cotton

shirt, I said, "I need to know about your downstairs neighbor."

"What about her?"

"Did you see much of her?"

His angular face squirmed into a very different smile. "I should say yes and no."

"Mr. Fallon?"

"If you mean do we talk much, the answer is no. She is, however, in the habit of sunbathing nude, so if that's what you mean, I've seen all there is."

"And she doesn't mind?"

"Apparently not. She lies out there every free moment during an entire week of every month. She's one of those olive-skinned women, and by the end of the week she has an all-over tan that any surfer would be proud of." He leaned back, and I didn't have to ask what picture was in his mind. "Doing that monthly can't be any good for her skin, but you'd never know it to look at her."

"You never go out or talk to her, or anything?" I asked in a tone of disbelief.

"Alas, I do have to keep my distance. I may be a Sri but I'm not a eunuch and hers is definitely not a body you'd kick out of bed. But I've moved the ashram eight times in the last year and a half, and I can't jeopardize this living arrangement for the benefit of my physical drives. Not everyone wants to live downstairs from chanters. And landlords rarely side with us when the neighbors complain."

"Hasn't Anne complained?"

"No. Before I moved in, I explained what we did, how we lived, how removed we were from other people, and she had no complaint. She's had none since. The perfect neighbor."

"Does she go out much?"

"She seems to keep regular work hours. She leaves at the time our morning devotions end."

"Do you chant then, too?"

"Oh, yes. Chanting interspersed with meditation."

"What time is that?"

"We start at six o'clock and end about eight."

I could see why I hadn't found an alarm clock in Anne's apartment. "What about at night?"

"I don't know. If I'm home there's usually something going on. I don't hear anything. It's our policy to keep to ourselves."

I sighed, regretting that if there had to be some religious person living upstairs from Anne, it couldn't be an aging fundamentalist who would watch her every movement lest some sin pass by unnoted.

"What about visitors?"

"She may have had them, but I saw very few; in fact, only one I can recall. A young man, with light-brown hair, lean build."

"How young?" Nat was nearly thirty.

Fallon shrugged.

"How tall was he? What about features—full or bony?"

But Fallon shook his head. "I saw the man only from above, and then only briefly each time."

"Recently?"

"Maybe once or twice a week for the past month."

"Did you see him last night?"

"I told you, Officer, I saw nothing outside the apartment after I got home."

"Okay, but I'll need the names of the people who were here then."

"I have no idea. I couldn't even give you descriptions. Once I get caught up in the Kirtan, that level of reality fades entirely."

I extracted a card. "Call me if you see or hear anything about Anne Spaulding."

He nodded, stood up, and turned on the tape.

Pushed by the roar of the Tibetan monks, I made my way down the stairs, feeling a more unstable mix of emotions than when I'd seen Anne's apartment. I would have to question Nat now. What was it with Nat? Why couldn't he just have told me the truth? Why did he go out of his way to tell me he'd never been inside Anne's apartment? His pen was in her living room, and the top of his head (or at least a head that fit his description) was a familiar sight to Sri Fallon. Why hadn't Nat told me?

Surely if Nat were involved in Anne's disappearance he wouldn't have called me. Unmentioned, it probably could have gone unreported for days. If her relations with the other neighbors were like that with Fallon, there would have been no report coming from there. From her office, perhaps. But it sounded like only Nat was very interested.

Whatever Nat's reason, it wouldn't be sufficient excuse. Shading the truth, hoping to avoid confrontation, was not a new tack with him. It reminded me why I'd divorced him.

But now I wondered if I could be detached enough to handle this investigation professionally. Regardless of Nat's peccadillos, his instincts were right. Something had happened to Anne Spaulding, something that needed investigation.

The sensible thing was to turn the case over to Howard. He knew almost as much as I did.

I walked back into Anne's apartment. Howard was coming from the kitchen. "Nothing in the backyard but weeds and ivy," he called, "and enough of them to keep Berkeley in compost till Christmas."

"Okay, lock it up."

Pereira headed toward the rear door.

With Howard, I started out the front. "Listen, I don't think—"

"What?" he yelled over the roar of the chant tape.

"About the case, you'd better—"

"Damn!" Howard ran to the curb.

"What is it?"

"My tail lights. The reflectors are gone. How am I going to explain this one?" Howard slumped against the car. "And the damned thing is that I set it up myself."

I put a hand on his arm, but he seemed unaware of it.

From the building the chant seemed to mock Howard: tail–lights–gone, tail–lights–gone.

Now I couldn't ask Howard to take the Spaulding case.

He had enough with the thefts, and if he didn't catch the thief, he wouldn't be driving around to handle anything.

The words of the chant seemed to change, to aim themselves at me: ques–tion–Nat, ques–tion–Nat.

Chapter

Leaving Anne Spaulding's other neighbors to Pereira, I rushed through the necessary procedures of getting a case number; dictating; running checks on Anne Spaulding and Ermentine Brown, the name I had found in Spaulding's wallet—checks that turned up nothing. I called the lab, on the unlikely chance that they were ahead of schedule, but their answer was as always: even for a Rush, their report on whether the bloodstains on the linen dress matched the samples taken from Anne's living room would reach me in no sooner than two or three days.

I dialed Nat's house, let the phone ring eight times. Nat didn't answer. It was nearly ten. He had said he'd be home by nine.

I slammed the receiver down. First he'd lied, and now he couldn't be bothered to stay home and find out what I'd discovered about Anne. In fact, if it had been so important to him, he could have walked over to Anne's while I was there; he'd said he was calling from a phone booth nearby. But he probably hadn't wanted to run into anyone who might have recognized him. And now most likely he was avoiding me.

I took a long, deep breath. I suspected I was going to be a lot angrier with Nat before this case ended.

There was almost an hour left on my shift. Everything in the case was on hold. I decided to check the only outside interest Anne's life had suggested: the wheelchair theater.

I drove west toward the freeway. Theater on Wheels was in that section of south Berkeley where small shingle houses gave way to factories and the low cement block buildings of exterminators or computer consultants. Residential fingers had stretched forth into the industrial area or industrial digits into the housing, so that it was not unusual to find three or four rundown post-Victorians between a shoe factory and a chemistry lab. During the day this area, with its scarred pavements and sidewalk-less yards, reminded me of the rural South. But at night the stark streetlights emphasized the darkness around them, the factories loomed larger in their emptiness and the little houses looked very vulnerable.

I wondered if the residents were pleased when one block of warehouses had been converted into artists' studios, crafts workshops, and the Theater on Wheels.

Theater on Wheels was in the middle of the block. Its stucco exterior had been painted English red and above the door hung a carved wooden sign identifying it. Beside the door a billboard advertised Ionesco's *Rhinoceros,* scheduled to open Friday.

The teasing half-light of closed shops shone from the artists' studios. Otherwise at ten-fifteen the street was as dark as any other nearby.

The theater too looked dark, but I tried the door anyway and was surprised to find it open.

Inside it was larger than I would have guessed, about the size of three classrooms. The stage occupied the far third.

It was easy to picture the building as it had been a few years back. Except for the addition of the stage, the the-

atrical lights suspended in seeming disarray from the
ceiling, and the green velvet curtain, little had been
changed. The English-red walls were still factory-like
and the rows of folding chairs gave the room an air of
transience. I had the feeling that as soon as I left, workmen would rush in, fold up the chairs, and replace them
with forty silk-screen machines.

I looked back at the stage. On it sat a lone man, his
wheelchair facing away from me, his head bent down as
if he were reading something on his lap.

As I approached, he turned the chair sharply, wheeled
to center stage, stopped abruptly and waited.

"I'm Officer Smith, Berkeley Police."

He eyed my uniform and, mocking my cadence, said,
"I'm Skip Weston, Theater Manager. And male lead in
Rhinoceros."

"Do you know Anne Spaulding?"

"Of course." He turned the chair toward the ramp at
the side of the stage and I accepted his unspoken invita-
tion to climb up.

Even at a distance his dark eyes had been piercing, as
if they had absorbed the life from his legs. But close up
they seemed to pulse, checking nervously to each side.

His body was marked by the contrasts common to
paraplegics—the bony knobs that lay where useful legs
had been, the muscled upper torso, and, in Weston's
case, a long, pallid face that might have suited a medi-
eval monk.

"Anne Spaulding," he said, "was supposed to be here
right now. There was a rehearsal scheduled tonight. I
had to send everyone home. We open in three days." He
glanced accusingly at the empty stage.

"And Anne didn't come at all?"

"No. No message, nothing." He stared at me again, and
it was as if the significance of my presence struck him
for the first time. "What's happened to her?"

"We don't know. She's missing."

"Missing?" His appraising tone suggested "missing"
wouldn't have been his first guess.

I waited for him to commit himself.

"What do you mean, 'missing?' " No commitment here.

"She's gone. Her belongings are still in her apartment."

"And what do you think happened?" He inched the chair forward.

"I told you, we don't know. What do *you* think?"

Now the chair moved across the stage and back—pacing. "Very unlike Anne."

"How so?"

"Missing is untidy. Anne, if anything, was organized, reliable, on top of things—yes, that's it, on top." He moved the chair quickly back and forth. "For instance, when Anne started with us two years ago, she had had some theater experience, in school, probably, but not much more than anyone else."

"She's an actress, then?"

"No, no. She's not chair-bound—that's the rule here—you can walk, or you can act, not both. Otherwise, we'd lose our grant. Stupid, isn't it? Damned hard to choreograph." He smiled, an expression out-of-synch with his tone. "There have been times, when six people were moving on stage, that it looked like the running of the bulls at Pamplona."

"So Anne just did your artwork?"

Now he laughed aloud.

I pulled out the yellow paper I'd found in Anne's apartment. Handing it to Weston, I said, "I found this preliminary sketch for the playbill in Anne's apartment."

Weston laughed harder. The light aluminum chair beneath him rocked precariously and I restrained the urge to reach for the armrests.

"Officer," Weston said, attempting to control himself, "this isn't a preliminary. This was Anne's final effort." He held out the sheet. "She's a talented woman. There's virtually nothing she doesn't know about—footlights, border-lights, floods, floorplans, props. She's done publicity, make-up, ticketing, you name it. What she didn't know she made it her business to learn." Again, he controlled the urge to laugh. "But, damn, she is one lousy, hopeless artist. Look at this. Even the printing looks like a third-grade project. And the sketch—it's closer to an amoeba than a rhinoceros." As he looked he gave up and laughed again. "In the end even Anne had to admit defeat."

There was an element of satisfaction in his final comment that made me ask, "Was that hard for her?"

"Damn it. It's hard for everyone. You must have led a very easy life if you don't know that."

I took a breath. "Was it harder for her than the average? I mean, do you think defeat was unusual for Anne?"

He closed his eyes a moment, as if he were channeling the power behind them. "I think," he said slowly, "it is one of the main things that separated her from us. Defeat was foreign to her. To us it's always lurking. Some of us fight it sporadically, some often, but defeat is always waiting."

"Defeat is always waiting for all of us," I said. "It's just in some cases the places it's hiding are less obvious."

He shrugged. Apparently he wasn't interested in my philosophizing.

I looked around for a chair. But, of course, there was none. All the actors brought their own. Leaning on the corner of a table, I said, "Tell me, what kind of person is Anne Spaulding?"

"I don't know."

"Haven't you been here long?"

He rolled the chair across the stage, turned and headed back, his uneven movements giving a thoughtful gait to his pacing. "Two years. I came right after Anne started working with the group."

"Two years, and you don't know her?"

He rolled to the far side of the stage and stopped. Facing me, he said, "I know what Anne Spaulding chose to display for us. But this is theater; we deal in facades."

"Was Anne good?"

"As a director? Yes. She had a particularly good sense of those nuances, phrases, movements that add a convincing touch. And she wasn't above learning—from ev-

eryone. She found out what each of us specialized in and
then she followed us around, hovered over us, literally,
until she knew as much as we did. Make-up is my thing,
and by now there's nothing I do that Anne couldn't
match—or nearly match."

"And did you find her attractive? I mean, men have."

He rolled, stopping less than a foot in front of me.
"Perhaps Anne put on a different act for other men. You
must realize, Officer, that when you are paralyzed, people tend to think of you as less than a man."

The bitterness of his words hung in the empty theater.
I swallowed and it sounded to me as if the swallow echoed against the walls. "Did Anne have any enemies?"

"If you mean did we resent her more than the rest of
ambulatory humanity—no. As a matter of fact, her distance, her lack of desire to help, was good. We cripples
are *helped* enough."

"Well, then did she have any special friends?" What
Weston said fit the woman who'd inhabited Anne's apartment, with the woman who'd lived beneath Sri Fallon—
it fit, but it left the person behind all that organization
and control unilluminated.

"She was friendly with Donn Day." He paused and
when I didn't react, said, "Don't you know 'Donn Day,
the Artist'? Donn—that's D-o-n-*n*— would be very put
out. I'm sure he feels his fame had descended even to the
ranks of constables."

I laughed. "That low, huh? What kind of friends were
Anne and Donn Day?"

Weston sidled the chair next to me. "Anne, as Anne,
seemed interested in his work, curious about him, the
artist. Donn, as Donn, was on the make."

"Successful?"

"Who knows? But my guess is that Donn would have
been much more likely to face defeat than Anne."

I glanced down at the notes I'd made. The name Donn
Day sounded familiar, but I couldn't think why. Maybe I
was more cultured than Weston thought. I asked, "What

would you speculate happened to Anne? She's probably been gone since last night."

"That's a long time to go for a walk."

"So?"

"Well," he said, rolling the chair back and forth in time with his phrasing, "I'd consider foul play, to put it in theatrical terms. I'd say kidnapping"—he stopped the chair—"or murder."

"Suspects?"

"None."

"Motive?"

"Again, a blank." He looked up, assessing me again. "But if you'd like to probe further, I'll take you out for a drink."

It was an offer that every woman cop I'd met had had, one that only the naive took as flattering. "If I do, I'll let you know."

I walked down the steps from the stage.

"I'll be around," Weston said, his actor's voice at once softly intimate, but carrying easily as I neared the back of the theater. "You may not recognize me, but I'll be around."

Chapter

7

I woke up groggy Wednesday morning. My landlord, Mr. Keppel, was trimming the hedge. In this north Berkeley neighborhood of small, tidy houses with small, tidy yards, it was not an unusual thing to be doing at ten-thirty. But that didn't make it any less annoying.

I hadn't slept well. Normally in an investigation like this I would have gone back to the station, waited for Howard, and talked. But last night I checked out before he could catch me. I didn't want to discuss this one, didn't want to explain Nat's considerable involvement in it, and didn't want Howard to offer to take it.

I had been tempted to go by Nat's house—he lived near me—but I wanted the control the phone would give. So I waited till I got home and tried his number. At quarter to twelve he was still out, or he'd turned off the phone bell. In either case, this investigation, which had been so important to him at six-thirty, had certainly lost its urgency by midnight. And I had gone to sleep with the intention of getting an early start and cornering him at work.

I sat up now, pulling the top of the sleeping bag

around my shoulders. Even on sunny mornings this room was cold.

I had been dreaming of Theater on Wheels. In the dream, it was still a factory filled with machines, machines making the whining sound of Mr. Keppel's mower. Now, staring down the length of the porch which the ever-economic Mr. Keppel had made into an apartment by putting indoor-outdoor carpet over the cement flooring, I could see why the previous incarnation of Theater on Wheels occurred to me. Indeed my "apartment" still was more porch-like than homey. Ten feet wide, it ran the width of the house, maybe forty feet. The interior wall was covered with white shingles and the three exterior ones with jalousies that opened into the backyard. Access to the yard for early spring sunbathing (a passion to anyone who grew up in the snow-covered East) was far and away the apartment's best feature.

It was possible that someone artistic, or even domestic enough to add curtains and pictures, might have created a home here, but my style of living had blended all-too-easily with Mr. Keppel's idea of conversion. In the year I'd lived here, I had added only a white wicker table, four straight chairs, and a floor lamp that shone down on the plastic chaise longue that really belonged in the yard.

And a couple of bookcases. They were relatively new acquisitions. For months the sight of paperbacks and hardcovers wedged into a bookcase had reminded me of Nat. (The first month after we'd separated I hadn't read so much as a newspaper.) But that passed. I'd retrieved my books, renewed my library card, and bought the shelves.

I wriggled out of the sleeping bag and headed into the kitchen that Mr. Keppel had created by halving his garage. Briefly I searched for a tea bag, gave up and turned on the shower. There were plenty of places that would serve me a better breakfast than I'd get here.

But after I showered it was too late to stop for breakfast. I drove directly to Anne's apartment, where I found

nothing changed, then hurried to the welfare office to
beat the lunchtime evacuation. It was eleven-forty-five
when I pulled up outside.

Although the sign said "Telegraph Office" the building
was half a block off Telegraph Avenue on a side street
that held small offices, restaurants, and apartments a
quarter-mile south of People's Park. Like several of its
neighbors, it was a one-story Victorian of a style common to the Bay Area. The door was on the left side and
behind it would be a long, narrow entryway that led at
the far end to a bathroom and pantry or laundry room.
From the entryway, on the right, an arch would open
into the parlor; behind the parlor would be the dining
room, behind that the kitchen, and another door would
lead from the kitchen to the pantry. The building looked
as if it was in original condition, complete with bay window and fluted trim, but the white paint was coated with
soot and only crab grass pushed through the cracked
clay soil in front. According to Nat, this building was a
sort of out-station to handle the Telegraph area.

I opened the door, expecting to find the place full, but
the entryway held only empty folding chairs. I stepped
in, and looked to my right, into what had once been the
front parlor. Now four interviewing booths—open-
topped plexiglass boxes—occupied most of the room,
two blocking the bay window and the others set in front
of the fireplace with a common wall dividing it. All were
empty. The built-in cabinets, eight-foot windows, and ca-
vetto cornices that had given the room its character were
now reduced to clutter impinging on the dull green lines
of the government's alterations.

It was in the next room behind it, the former dining
room, that I spotted a mountainous dark-haired woman
in a red caftan seated at a government-issue desk beneath an oil painting. It was an abstract in various
shades of blue, signed a bit too largely and clearly—
Donn Day. It was hard to say which was the more arresting, the painting or the woman.

As I walked in, she turned in her chair, noted my uniform and eyed me suspiciously.

In Berkeley the police enjoyed good relations with social workers and eligibility workers. I was surprised at this unspoken hostility.

"Can I help you?" she asked. The dark hair was gathered at the nape of the neck and hung down her back. Her eyes were heavily outlined and shadowed in green; lipstick that had started out red had been eaten away with just traces of its original shade surviving at the corners of her mouth. Whatever image she had hoped the make-up would project was overshadowed by the sagging flesh of her jowls and chin.

Nat had started work here after our separation. I had had no reason to meet his co-workers and, knowing Nat, I was sure if he'd mentioned having an ex-wife at all, he would never have admitted she was a cop.

"I'm looking for Nat Smith," I said.

"He's gone for the day."

"Gone for the day, already!"

"To a meeting in Oakland," she said. "They've all gone. The meeting starts at one. They left early to allow time for lunch and travel."

"And the meeting lasts all afternoon, then?"

"It's scheduled to. In any case, they certainly won't be back here today."

I sighed, allowing myself to sink down on the folding chair behind me. The fat woman turned over the manila folder she had been writing in, name side down, then swivelled to face me.

Meeting her gaze, I said, "Perhaps you can help me anyway."

"Now?" She placed a hand protectively atop the manila folder.

"What's wrong with now?"

"I'm waiting for a client."

"At ten to twelve?"

"Oh, yes. She works. Some of our clients do. I didn't want her to take time off. And, besides, it's so much quieter here at lunchtime. It's so difficult to talk about emotional problems with all the turmoil during the day."

I felt certain Nat had told me that in this office they dealt only with eligibility. Still, I asked, "You're an eligibility worker, aren't you? I thought eligibility workers dealt with money, and social workers handled problems."

"They do, but, except for protective cases, where social workers are always assigned, clients have one only if they request it. Every client has an eligibility worker to take care of finances, and many of us have every bit as much training as social workers."

Offering no comment on that, I said, "I'm investigating the disappearance of Anne Spaulding. What can you tell me about her, Ms. . . ."

"Day. Fern Day."

"Are you any relation . . . ?" I looked up at the canvas on the wall over her desk.

She followed my gaze to the blue abstract painting. "To Donn? Yes, my husband."

"It has a nice feel," I said.

"Thank you. It's not one of Donn's best. But it would be sacrilege to hang fine art in here."

I couldn't help but agree with Fern Day. Along with shelves set back-to-back, five desks were crammed into the dining room, three by the windows and the others along the inside wall. Hard light flowed from fluorescent fixtures and notices and clippings were Scotch-taped in a haphazard fashion above the other desks.

"About Anne?" I prompted. "She's been missing since some time before you came to work yesterday."

"Missing. Yes." She rolled the words around on her tongue as if tasting the possibilities they held. Her whole expression showed more intrigue than worry. "We can talk here for a few minutes while I wait for Mrs. . . . for the client. Confidentiality, you know."

I opened my pad, wondering what Fern Day thought I might do with this valuable client's name. And if the woman arrived while I was here, would she enter in disguise? "Where is Anne's family?"

"She never mentioned any. She's not the family type."

"What was her full name?"

"Her middle name was a last name—Martin? Marvin? Something like that. I know it began with M because she had a purse with her initials on it."

"And a dress?"

"Yes. She wore it Monday. Why do you ask?"

"Would you recognize it again?"

Without hesitation Fern said, "Yes. I have a good visual sense. I *am* an artist's wife."

I arranged for her to stop by the station and have a look at the bundle of clothes found by the Bay. Taking out my notepad, I asked, "Who are Anne's friends?"

"Besides the men here?"

"Not excluding them. Was she particularly close to someone here?"

"I think she knew Alec Effield, our supervisor, before she started here, and of course she did train Nat Smith. He's a graduate student, been here only about a year." Fern looked at the name on my pocket. I asked quickly, "Who did she see outside of work?"

I could almost see the speculations lining up behind her eyebrows. "I'm afraid I don't know. Anne doesn't tell me about her private life."

I asked about Anne's enemies, but seemingly the informational blackout had been total. "Can you think of any reason she would have left so suddenly?"

Fern's finger went to her mouth. It was a tapered finger on a long graceful hand, a hand that looked as if it were on the wrong body. "No, I can't. Poor Alec's just been swamped, trying to take care of her cases. It was so inconsiderate of Anne. But then Anne's not really a thoughtful person."

"She's been inconsiderate?"

"I wouldn't want to say that." She paused. "Don't think that I don't like Anne; it's just that she's, well, rather immature in some areas." Fern leaned forward. "Anne hasn't really learned to care about other people. It's not that she dislikes people as much as that she's oblivious to their needs. It doesn't occur to her to put herself out." She sighed. "Anne would never see a client at lunch."

"Didn't Anne get on with her clients, then?"

Fern bit the finger. "I didn't say that."

I waited while Fern went through a string of circumlocutions to arrive at the conclusion that there was no reason Anne's clients should have liked her but no proof to the contrary. "Of course," she said, "Anne has more variety in her caseload—some families, a lot of single adults, and a number of clients who have part-time jobs— they're street artists on Telegraph, waitresses, or such."

Glancing at the cluttered green desks, I asked, "Which is Anne's?"

"None of these. Anne's desk is in the back."

I stood up. Following my example, Fern raised herself and led me through the kitchen—now converted to a one-desk office—to what had been a laundry room.

"Anne's," she said.

The regulation metal desk stood where the big sinks had been. The room was small, dingy, and cold. Despite the desk and chair, it still looked like a laundry room. I wondered what Alec Effield had had against Anne to assign her to this place.

I was about to ask when a woman's voice called, "Mrs. Day?"

Fern turned.

Taking advantage of her need to rush, I said, "Where were you Monday evening?"

"That's a strange question," she said, looking toward the door. "I thought Anne was missing."

"Missing can cover a lot of ground."

"You mean it could be more serious?"

I nodded.

"She could be . . ." There was a long pause as if Fern were seeking a euphemism for the ultimately unpleasant word: ". . . dead?"

"We don't know."

Fern bit down on the flesh below her lower lip so that the center of the lip itself was entirely hidden by her teeth. Slowly she let the lip back out. "That's terrible. Poor Anne," she said without emotion. "Why would someone kill Anne?"

I made a mental note of her interpretation of murder rather than suicide.

"Mrs. Day?" The woman sounded closer.

Recalling my question, I asked, "Monday night?"

"I was at home." She glanced nervously toward the door.

"Did you go out at all?"

"Oh, no. Donn told me about his day—who he saw, what his ideas were, what innovations he was considering in his work—" She looked past me to the door.

I stepped back, and Fern rushed from the room.

Fern Day had set up an alibi for Donn and for herself. There was something she wasn't telling me but I didn't have enough information to decide where to press yet. Whatever Fern's secret, it, and the presence of her waiting client, had sufficiently unnerved her so that she'd abandoned Anne's office. I was willing to bet that under normal circumstances she would have stood her ground here against the entire Berkeley police force.

I stood a moment, glancing around Anne's office. The walls sported neither pictures nor notices; peels of beige paint hung from the ceiling. Welfare manuals were stacked in piles on the desk; uncovered ballpoint pens lay around them. On the left side was a folder marked "To Do" and in it lists headed "Renewals," "Address Changes," and "Closings." All the names on the lists had been crossed out. Anne must have been very efficient.

I checked the desk, and found it divided, as Anne's apartment had been, into the messy and the meticulous. In the first of the three left-side drawers were jumbles of cups, tea bags, maps, and phone books, and in the other two, carefully ordered groups of agency memos, work forms, and folders. The folders stood in the deep-bottomed drawer in alphabetical order by the client's name.

On a hunch I checked for Ermentine Brown. Maybe she was a welfare client and the "20" had something to do with her case. But if so, her case wasn't here.

I was just about to shut the drawer when I spotted more folders in a heap at the back. They were much thinner than the others. I pulled them out and opened the first, aware that this was illegal. I'd need a warrant to do it right. The first folder held four legal-size forms. One form gave identifying information—name, address, social security number, marital status; on another Anne had written "O/V" and two dates within the past month. The remaining forms appeared to be some sort of financial worksheets.

The second folder contained the same, plus a few long, brown, curly hairs—obviously not Anne Spaulding's hair —lying amongst the papers. By the third folder I realized I had no idea what was supposed to be recorded here and what wasn't, and I could hardly ask Fern Day to explain.

I satisfied myself with making a list of the names— seventeen in all. There were five sizeable families with addresses in two buildings off Telegraph, and twelve single women, who lived in Telegraph-area hotels. One of the hotels was the place I'd chased Howard's thief through.

Four of Anne's clients lived at that hotel. Perhaps I'd have a talk with them and find out why Anne had separated out their folders. And I'd have another talk with Quentin Delehanty.

Replacing the folders, I made my way back to the room with the five desks and the shelves of case folders. Glancing around the corner I could see the outline of Fern Day in one of the plexiglass booths. Her client's voice was soft, the phrasing hesitant. Fern sat unmoving, as if entranced.

I pulled open the top file drawer, but, though there were numerous Browns, there were no Ermentines.

I slipped back into the kitchen. It, too, was now an office, but with a greater complement of green metal government furniture. The supervisor's office. Notices were tacked in rows at either side of a bulletin board. In the middle was a pen-and-ink print—Suzanne Valadon's "After the Bath." And on the supervisor's desk directly beneath it lay a half-done copy, a very good copy. Presumably Alec Effield, the supervisor here, had a fair amount of free time.

Behind the desk was a file shelf half the size of the one in the next room. It was marked "Closed files."

It didn't take me long to find Ermentine Brown's folder and take down her address and the date her welfare grant had been discontinued because of—if my interpretation of the crabbed writing that could only have been Anne's was correct—excess income.

A closed case—reason to resent Anne? Ermentine Brown could tell me herself.

Chapter

On the off chance that he might have detoured by the house on the way to his meeting, I called Nat there. He hadn't.

Ravenous, I stopped at Wally's Donut Shop and ordered eggs and sausage. Lowering the platter, Wally glanced from the eggs to the hash browns and sausage and up at me. "This is big time for you, isn't it? I thought you only ate jelly donuts."

"This is breakfast."

"Good thing. Most important meal. Though"—he wiped a hand across his apron—"a lot of people eat breakfast in the morning."

"Wally," I said, "I'm doing the best I can."

He grinned. It was a variation on an old interchange. Wally's was close to the station and many a break had been spent here, many a jelly donut consumed, and many a cup of coffee that should rightfully have been tossed out had washed down those donuts. I salted everything, poured ketchup over the eggs and hash browns, and forked off a piece of scrambled egg.

My thoughts were on the case. What did I know, so
far? Anne Spaulding had been missing for a day and a
half. Her apartment looked like it had been the scene of
a fight. So presumably, she had fought someone and
. . . and lost. If she'd won she would have been home
and I'd have been taking my complaint from her. So
she'd lost.

Who was that someone? A psychotic killer who had
chosen her at random, dumped her bloody clothes by the
Bay and done . . . what? . . . with her nude body? A
sex killing? If so, the killer would go on attacking
women month after month or week after week until we
could collect enough data to track him down. How many
women would die before then?

I spread strawberry jam on my toast. Once, thoughts
of murder had knotted my stomach, but now I could
consider what would make a normal person retch and
not miss a bite.

Suppose the killer were not psychotic, not random.
Suppose it was someone she knew . . . a friend? So far
that meant Nat or Alec Effield, the supervisor. Anne
didn't seem to put herself out to make friends, if Skip
Weston and Fern Day were to be believed. And what of
Nat's pewter pen in Anne's living room? I knew how
much he valued that pen. I knew how careful Nat was.
The pen wasn't something he would mislay, unless . . .
but I couldn't picture him there while the blood was still
fresh.

I'd have to get this issue of the pen cleared up soon. It
could provide a wedge to force Nat to describe Anne's
life much more thoroughly than he apparently wanted.
And I certainly had to have an explanation of Nat and
the pen before Lt. Davis read about it in my initial report.

The only other lead was "Ermentine Brown 20," the
notation I had found in Anne's wallet, the former welfare client whose case had been closed for excess income. I finished the hash browns, paid Wally, ignoring

his reproof about the scarcely touched eggs, and headed for my car.

Ermentine Brown lived in public housing. Her unit was at the end of what appeared to be a giant stucco shoebox. Before it, the grass had been trampled and the hard clay soil shone through.

The shades of her apartment were drawn, but the unmistakable crescendos of a soap opera told me someone was home. I pushed the bell.

The door was opened by a small child. She had six pigtails and wore pink pajamas that had attached feet. As she looked at me, her face scrunched in displeasure.

"Momma, there's a cop at the door."

I could hear water running and the pans banging. In the living room two older children sat leaning against a threadbare brown couch, the light from the television shining on their motionless faces. A tissue box sat between them. October, and already it was flu season.

In a minute a black woman with a large Afro approached. Her hands went to her hips. "Yeah?"

"I'm Officer Smith, Berkeley Police. Are you Ermentine Brown?"

"Why you want to know?"

I repeated the question. The child moved behind her mother.

"Yeah, I'm Ermentine Brown. So?"

"Do you know Anne Spaulding?"

"Miss Spaulding from the welfare? Yeah, I sure as hell know her. Something bad happen to her?"

"She's missing."

Ermentine Brown's eyebrows shot up. "Don't say!" Her tired face pushed into a smile.

Taking advantage of her mood, I said, "Do you mind if I come in?"

She led me through the small living room to a kitchen of approximately the same size. The walls were pinky beige, the furniture Goodwill, and the aroma, spaghetti sauce.

She moved to a half-empty coffee cup at the table.

I sat. "Was Anne Spaulding your eligibility worker?"

"Right."

"Why did you choose to go off welfare?"

"Choose! Woman, I didn't choose nothin'! That bitch, that Spaulding bitch, didn't count my work expenses. She said I had too much income. From selling feather necklaces! Too goddamned much money from feathers!" She flung up her hands.

"You're a street artist on Telegraph?"

"Yeah, I'd be up there now if it weren't for all these sick kids."

"So Anne Spaulding counted your income, and you weren't eligible?"

Her chin jutted out. "No way. *She* said I wasn't eligible. Any straight worker would have taken off for my supplies. Feathers are free only to birds. But that bitch Spaulding didn't count nothin'."

"Couldn't you have appealed her decision?"

"Yeah, I could have if I wanted to wait six months for a verdict. If I had the time to go down to Legal Aid and wait around to see a free lawyer. If I had the time to go to the hearing. And if I'd got the paper in ten days. They only give you ten days to appeal those things. If the letter gets held up in the mail, too bad. You understand?"

"Ermentine Brown 20" became clearer now. "So you decided to bribe Anne Spaulding?"

"What? You foolin' with me? You see those kids in there. You think I got extra money to give away? You think they don't eat, huh?"

I waited for a moment before I said, "We've got a note in her writing. It was twenty dollars, wasn't it?"

"No way." Ermentine Brown grabbed a piece of paper and put down a big zero. "Now you got my note, see."

"You're forcing me to take you in and show you the proof." When she didn't reply I continued, "Look, Ms. Brown, I'm not interested in going after you for twenty dollars. I will if necessary, but what I really want is information. I think we can work something out."

"Go ahead. I'm listening."

A pigtail poked around the corner. I watched as the rest of the head inched after it. "We won't be long," I said to the child.

Ermentine Brown spun in her chair, ready to let her tension out, but the child darted back into the living room.

When the woman turned back to me, I said, "What made you think you could bribe Anne Spaulding?"

She hesitated. "The word's out on the Avenue. She's on the take."

"Who else was she taking from?"

She shrugged. "I don't know names."

I pulled out my pad, flipping to the page on which I had listed the seventeen case names. I read them. "Any of these women?"

"No. I never heard of them."

"They live right off Telegraph. They go to the same branch welfare office. And you're telling me you've never heard of them?"

Ermentine stood up. "Look, woman, I lived up there for a month, in a hotel full of winos and whores. If I knew any of those names I'd tell you and let you go hang all over them."

"Well, then, who else was bribing Anne Spaulding? Only you? Anne Spaulding is missing and I need to know what she was doing."

"If there's any way that bitch could get her ass kicked there's no one would like to see it more than me. I told her the day she cut me off, my kids needed that money, I couldn't put food in their mouths without it. And you think she cared? Shit."

"The names."

"I know some people who used to be into it, but not now. Look, why don't you talk to Quentin Delehanty up on the Avenue? He's a wise dude when he's off the sauce."

"When's that?"

For the second time Ermentine Brown smiled.

" 'Tween the time his eyes open and his hand reaches out."

I laughed. "One more thing. Where were you last Monday from six o'clock on?"

I expected her to protest, but she didn't. Instead she went to the living room and returned with a large plastic purse. Sitting down, she began rooting through the purse, pulling out envelopes stuffed with papers and stacking them in a line on the formica table. "I fed the kids and then I took them to see the Marx Brothers. I'm finding the stubs so you can be sure."

"You saved the stubs!"

"Listen, once you been on the welfare, you save everything. You don't never know what they're going to ask for." She looked up and caught me staring at the purse. "I call this my file cabinet. When you been on the welfare you keep your papers handy. You never know when you're going to be in the office and they'll have to have something right now! You learn to keep everything in it." She patted the purse. "You check with anyone on the welfare. They all do it."

She turned her attention back to the purse and in a minute came up with an envelope that contained the theater stubs. "Here, you can still see the date."

I glanced at them and returned them to the envelope, which Ermentine Brown returned promptly to her purse. "Ms. Brown, can you think of anyone who would want to harm Anne Spaulding?"

Her eyes widened, her mouth opened, and she laughed. "Anyone she met, honey. Ain't no one gonna be crying over her."

Chapter

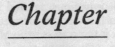

I got to the station at twenty to three. In the past I'd been late for or even missed squad meetings and Lt. Davis, a stickler for time and accuracy, had wasted none of the former letting me know that no investigation excuses a patrol officer from basic responsibilities. I was going to have a hard enough time explaining this case to the lieutenant without adding lateness to my irregularities.

Pereira's report was in. Spaulding's neighbors had noticed nothing unusual or helpful. They could remember neither friends nor visitors. Mostly they used the opportunity to complain about the traffic and the noise from Sri Fallon's apartment. Anne they classified as a nice quiet neighbor who kept to herself.

I arranged for Fern Day to view the clothes. Then I checked the microfilm index on which we kept the names of all those—felons and victims—known to the Department, together with the number of the Penal Code section identifying the crime each was connected with. There was no record for any of Anne's twelve adult welfare clients or her five family cases.

And then I got the first good news in two days: Lt. Davis was at City Hall, meeting with the mayor.

Staff meeting was perfunctory: a memo on expense accounts was read, the hot-car list circulated, summaries of cases left over from Morning Watch presented. But the atmosphere was not the same. We were like a school class with a substitute teacher. Howard, who normally forced himself to be serious, leaned back in his chair, arms spreading out, unconsciously forcing the men on either side to give him room. The loss of a '62 VW without bumpers, but with one red, one green, and two merely rusted fenders gave rise to speculation that would not have been so much as suppressed thoughts if the lieutenant had been present.

"Another day," Howard said after the meeting. He flopped back in my desk chair, spreading his long legs across the aisle. "Thank God I don't have to explain about my tail lights till tomorrow."

"So what do you have planned for the thief today?" I settled atop the desk.

"Nothing. The pattern is no contact the day after a grab—and he had two tries yesterday. Today I'd guess he's holed up somewhere slobbering over his latest trophy. What about your missing person?"

"Not much, except a general opinion that Anne Spaulding knew how to look out for Number One. And Number Two, if such existed, was a long way down the list. She had some welfare clients living in that building I chased your thief through. I'm going to go out and have a crack at them." I pushed myself up. "Could you do me a favor and check by Anne's apartment when you're on beat? It'd be a little humiliating to have her just walk home without my knowing."

"Sure. What does your husband—whoops, ex-husband —think happened?"

I was a few feet down the aisle. "I'll tell you about that later, okay?"

*   *   *

It was not yet four o'clock. The sun still warmed Telegraph and there was no sign of fog yet. The Avenue was
jammed with people; after the cold Bay Area summer,
people exposed their bodies greedily to the warm October sun. In a few hours, when the fog rolled in, they'd be
wrapped in sweaters or wool jackets, but now T-shirts
and shorts prevailed.

I double-parked the car outside Quentin Delehanty's
hotel and made my way past the empty lobby. The smell
of marijuana hung heavy; the bald rugs and thin curtains
had been saturated with it. There was no sign of the hotel manager, no manager's office. The manager, doubtless, was someone who came by only when the rent was
due.

There were no mailboxes, though a few unclaimed letters lay on a table, and no list of tenants. No one was
around to guide me. I knocked on the back door—Delehanty's. From inside I could hear nothing. The blare of
stereos from other rooms was louder than the television
had been at Ermentine Brown's.

I knocked again. Now I could make out stirrings.

"Open the door, Delehanty. It's the police."

Grunts.

It was several minutes and two more poundings before the door opened to reveal Delehanty in a wine-
stained and very dirty white shirt and pajama bottoms.
His long gray hair was matted around his face and he
smelled of wine and sweat.

Taking a breath, I walked in. Delehanty watched me,
his expression more amazed than angry.

I took out a list of Anne Spaulding's clients, and read
the names slowly. "Do you know any of these women?"

His head shook in a mechanical motion.

"Four of them live right here, in this hotel."

"Who?" Delehanty's voice was hoarse.

"Linda Faye Miller, Amelia Sanders, Yvonne McIvor,
and Janis Ulrick."

Delehanty's head shook. "Nope."

"Nope what?"

"Don't live here. Never heard of them."

"They've never lived here?" I asked.

"Not since I've been here, and that's over a year."

"You sure?"

"Yeah. I know who's here. Either they're down here bitching about me, or I'm up there telling them to keep their goddamned rock music from blowing out my eardrums."

I couldn't help but think that this hotel was an unfortunate choice for someone who objected to noise. "Why don't you move?"

"On two hundred dollars a month? Maybe I could go to San Francisco and stay at the Fairmont?" He reached under the bed and came up with a wine bottle, an empty. He stared, then dropped it.

"You're only getting General Assistance—county money? Why don't you apply for Social Security?"

"Hey, lady, I'm not disabled."

I looked pointedly at the bottle, but Delehantly avoided my stare.

"I don't drink all the time. It's just that, well, one of the guys here died over the weekend. O.D.'d. He was just a kid. Tad. Just twenty-one. I warned him. I told him to watch it. I—" He stared down at the streaked floor. His eyes began to unfocus.

"Before I go," I said, "just one more thing. Do you know Anne Spaulding?"

His eyes shot open. His face reddened. "Spaulding! Do I know that Spaulding bitch! The bitch at welfare? She's the one. She made Tad do it. If she'd left him alone he'd be alive today. She did it. She killed him." His face was red; his fists banged on the bed.

"What did she do?"

"Cut him off, that's what. She cut him off. Tad got the notice last Thursday. No more money. He freaked. Just twenty-one. Jesus!"

"Did you know Anne Spaulding yourself?"

"What? Yeah, I know who she is. Everyone knows. You

don't do something like that and remain anon . . . anon
. . . unknown."

"You're still pretty angry, aren't you?"

Delehanty stared at me in disgust. "Don't give me that
social work crap—still pretty angry. Tad's still pretty
dead."

I wasn't getting anyplace with that line of questioning.
"Who lives here?"

"You want who's in all twenty rooms? Hell, I can't tell
you that. Look at the register, lady. And leave me alone.
I've got some serious drinking to do."

"Where were you Monday night, Delehanty?"

"What? Go away."

"I will when you answer me. Where were you?"

"Here. Where do you think? You think you get this
hung over by just drinking for an hour? You want to see
the proof?" He didn't wait for my reply, but pulled back
the bedcovers and displayed six boxes filled with empty
wine bottles under the bed.

Obviously they were more than this week's collection,
but there seemed no point in pressing it. I asked for wit-
nesses, but Delehanty maintained he hadn't gone out of
his room.

Strange that all the people involved with Anne were
such homebodies.

As I left, Delehanty's head sunk to his hands. He
reached for a bottle of aspirin. And I wondered how long
it would be before he joined his friend Tad.

Making a mental note to find the hotel manager and
get a list of tenants, I headed back to the car and sat
there, examining what I had learned.

There was no reason not to believe Ermentine Brown's
story that Anne was extracting bribes from street vendors. There was no reason for Delehanty to insist the
women on the list never stayed at the hotel—feigning
ignorance would have been easier. But if those clients
did not live here, where were they and why had Anne
separated out their case folders? Were they living elsewhere and bribing Anne to say they lived here? It didn't

make much sense, but there was something going on with those missing clients and it was the only lead I had —except for Nat's pen.

I wondered what Alec Effield, Anne's supervisor, knew about it.

Chapter

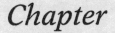

I checked back at the welfare department in case Alec Effield had returned. He hadn't, a disgruntled Fern Day told me between the ringing of two phones.

My next stop was at the station to run a quick make on Effield. While I waited, I dialed Nat and listened to the phone ring eight times. He had asked me to start this investigation. He had said to let him know. Dammit, where was he?

The microfilm had no listing for Alec Effield—no crimes, no complaints. I got his address and headed for a car.

Rush hour. None of the cross-town streets was more than four lanes wide. Grove Street, with parking on both sides, was effectively two-lane, but it was still predominately residential and I could make better time on it. Even so, it took me twenty minutes to cross most of north Berkeley and turn east into the hills.

In reality the Berkeley hills are not individual peaks but a long bulge on the eastern edge of the Hayward Fault from Contra Costa County in the north almost to

San Jose in the south. The streets wind steeply upward,
overhung by branches of live oak and liquid amber, and
lined by four-bedroom houses clustered close together.
Turning north just short of the summit, I wondered how
a welfare supervisor could afford a house here.

But Alec Effield turned out not to live in a house. He
had a flat over the garage, ten feet to the left of a large,
dark, Queen Anne house. The brick steps to Effield's flat
matched the curved walkway to the main house. The
yard showed signs of a flower garden recently pulled up.
The grass was cut, the edges trimmed.

As I climbed Effield's steps, I could hear the sounds of
Ravel.

I knocked and when the door opened, identified myself.

Soft light, soft music flowed up behind the man who,
in turn, identified himself as Alec Effield, giving him the
aura of a celestial character from a Busby Berkeley mu-
sical. His eyes were the palest blue and his flaxen hair
was barely distinguishable from his gently tanned face,
his beige turtleneck, and beige slacks. But as he asked
why I was there, his voice was jarring. He had the last
vestige of a New York accent, and even it sounded faded.
In another year or two he would blend perfectly into his
beige surroundings.

Waving me inside, he turned off the music and turned
on an art deco lamp. The brighter light showed a carefully understated room; the only signs of use were two
indentations close together on a toffee-colored love seat.
Whoever was responsible for the second depression was
not visible.

I decided on a direct approach. "I'm afraid Anne
Spaulding may be dead. We found clothing that appears
to be hers by the Bay."

Effield gasped, a timid sound.

I waited, giving him time to recover. "I'm sure you
want to help us."

"Yes, of course. It's awful. Anne?"

"Did she have any enemies?"

"Not that I know of."

"Kinky friends?"

"Oh, no. Not Anne."

"We don't have much to go on, but we do know she was accepting bribes from her clients."

Effield's pale eyes opened wider. He looked around, as if hoping his friend would emerge suddenly and answer for him. "Surely, Officer, surely that couldn't be true."

"I'm afraid it is. It's common knowledge."

"But that's not possible. I would have heard if Anne had done anything like that. Ours is a small office. Perhaps if you'd seen it—"

"I've been there."

Effield lifted a brass letter opener from the end table and moved his fingers precisely back and forth along the sides of the blade, carefully avoiding the sharp edges. "You say it's common knowledge. You have people who will swear that Anne took money from her clients?"

"Yes." *Maybe* was closer to the truth.

Effield shook his head. "This is awful. Nothing like this has ever happened in our office. I just can't believe it." He put the letter opener back on the end table. "But I suppose it must be. I just wouldn't have thought it of Anne." He groaned. "This is terrible. I vouched for her. She used me as a reference. What will they think?"

"You knew Anne back East, is that right?"

"Yes. In New York."

"How did you come to know her there?"

"We both worked for the welfare department. She was there briefly, only a few months. But she had completed training. She did know the job." He seemed anxious that I see the validity of his recommendation.

"And were you friends in New York?"

Effield seemed to consider this. "Acquaintances. I lost track of Anne after she left the department, and then I ran into her right before I came out here. She followed, well, not followed, but she came here later and she knew I'd be at the department here and she called and asked to use me as a reference."

A toilet flushed. I flipped a page in my notes. There was a lot of ground I needed to cover before we were interrupted. "Then there are Anne's clients who don't live where they're supposed to."

Effield looked up, startled.

I was on shakier ground here. "Mr. Effield, Anne has twelve adult cases with addresses at three Telegraph Avenue hotels."

"Yes," Effield said slowly, "we do have clients living in hotels."

"These women don't. I've already checked one hotel and none of them lives there. No one remembers them. There's nothing to say they exist."

Effield sat.

Water splashed in what I supposed was the bathroom.

"Oh," he said.

The water stopped. A door at the back of the room opened a crack.

"This is overwhelming. First you tell me Anne's dead, then you say she was accepting bribes, and now you say her cases have the wrong addresses." Effield's head shook ever more slowly. Finally he said, "I'm trying to think how that could be. Perhaps, yes, perhaps Anne was in the process of changing their addresses. You see, Officer, a lot of clients are transients of sorts. They come to Berkeley and they need to have an address in order to apply for aid, so they live at one of those hotels where it's easy to find a room cheap and the management asks no questions. A lot of places won't rent to welfare recipients."

"But they don't live there, Mr. Effield."

"I'm getting to that." Now he seemed quite confident, protected by his bureaucratic knowledge. "As soon as aid is granted, the client can look for another place, and those hotels being what they are, most people move on quickly. So what you saw are, no doubt, people who've moved and notified the department of their change of address."

"Can you show me any proof of that?"

"I don't know. What type of thing did you have in mind?" He seemed uneasy. He swallowed, then looked directly at me. "Nat Smith's worked with Anne. He should know what went on in her cases. Maybe you should ask him."

In spite of my nametag, Effield didn't make the connection and for once I was profoundly thankful for a common name. To Effield, I said, "I will be talking to all the workers, but right now I need evidence. The case folders must have some listing of the new addresses. I could run down the clients, if they exist."

"All of them?"

"It depends on time."

"Well, the thing is, Officer, I *am* bound by the rules of confidentiality. Much as I'd like to get this straightened out, I just can't reveal the addresses of twelve clients, not even to the police. I could be fired for a breach like that."

"I see. You've got your rules. I could get a court order—" I let the statement hang, hoping it would bring forth some offer. It was a threat I didn't want to have to carry out—one I doubted I could get approved.

The bathroom door opened and a woman started out. I caught her eye and shook my head.

Effield had been too involved in his thoughts to notice. "Suppose," he said, "I can arrange for you to see one of those clients. I could find out if one of them would be willing to talk to you."

I considered that, picturing Effield meticulously going through the stack, choosing the least offensive client. "No, that's not good enough. Not representative."

He sat, his eyes nearly closed, so that his whole body seemed devoid of color. His eyes opened and his gaze lifted till he nearly met my eyes. "Why don't you choose the client?"

"I still don't like you arranging it."

"I'm afraid there's no other way within our rules."

Picturing Lt. Davis' exasperated expression as I discussed a court order, I said, "Okay." And glancing through the list I had copied, I chose a name from Delehanty's hotel, one I knew didn't live there. "How about Yvonne McIvor?"

"Yvonne McIvor?" the woman behind Effield asked in a listless voice. "Who's that?"

Effield turned. It was a moment before he said, "I'd forgotten you were here. This is Mona Liebowitz," he added to me. I recalled Mona Liebowitz's name from the desk next to Fern Day's.

Mona took a sluggish step into the room. In a stained T-shirt and long faded skirt she looked like something Alec Effield would use to wax his car. She had broad features and long curly brown hair that hung to the tip of her shoulder blades. But her most attention-grabbing feature, behind which all others blurred, were the large loose breasts that strained her cotton shirt. I, who am built like a Cub Scout, stared. Effield failed miserably in his attempt to direct his eyes elsewhere.

Recalling the indentations on the sofa, I wasn't surprised that Effield had seemed distracted.

Mona lowered herself to the couch, pulling her bare and dirty feet up under her.

Ignoring Effield's muffled gasp, she said, "So who is Yvonne McIvor?"

"One of Anne's clients."

"I don't—"

"Mona," Effield said, "I'm breaking the rules of confidentiality as it is. I don't want to discuss this more than necessary." To me, he added, "I'll arrange what we discussed tomorrow."

"Fine," I said. "I'll be at your office at eight-thirty." Eight-thirty was way before I wanted to begin work, but I couldn't give Effield time to call Yvonne McIvor before I arrived.

Effield stood up. "I hope this finishes it."

"I hope it will," I said. "But I do need one more piece of information from you."

"What? Surely—"

"Not about your clientele."

"Oh." Effield seemed to waver between remaining

erect and slumping onto the sofa. Automatically he
glanced at his hand and, presumably finding it clean,
used it to brace himself against the light fabric.

"What I need to know, Mr. Effield, is where you were
Monday night."

He looked so startled and relieved that I wondered
what he had been expecting me to ask.

"Here," he said.

"All evening?"

"Yes. I came directly from work. I never left."

"Can anyone verify that? It's not that I doubt your
word, but we do need—"

"Oh, yes." He smiled. "Mona was here."

I shifted my glance to her, still lounging against the far
end of the sofa.

"I'm the perfect alibi," she said with an amused grin
that seemed to vivify her entire body. "I rode here with
Alec right from work, so that was about five-thirty that
we arrived. And I left around nine-thirty or ten."

"Alec drove you home?"

"Yes." She smiled again, mostly with her eyes, as if
some private thought—ironic, unkind, scandalous—had
emerged.

"Was there anything you wanted to add?"

"No." She stretched, unshaven legs pushing out from
her loose cotton skirt. "If you're leaving," she said lan-
guidly, "maybe you could give me a lift down the hill."

Effield opened his mouth, but he must have thought
better of his protest. Perhaps his mental picture, too, was
focused on driving Mona home Monday night.

"Mr. Effield," I said.

"Yes." He looked wary and annoyed, as if I had again
gone back on my word about the last question.

"When you drove Mona home, did you go in?"

"No. I dropped her in front of the driveway."

"And then?"

"Then?"

"I mean, did you go anywhere else, or come on home?"

"Home."

"And what time did you get back here?"

"I don't know. For goodness' sakes, Officer . . ."

"If he left me at ten," Mona said, "he would have been back here before ten-thirty. It's only a twenty-minute drive."

"Do you concur, Mr. Effield?" I felt as if I were dealing with a deaf person, having to write out every question and wait while each minimal answer was spelled out in response.

"Yes."

I closed my notepad. Effield retrieved a velvet cloak from the closet and slipped it over Mona's shoulders as she lifted her long, curly hair. Whatever their relationship, it was apparent that Effield was willing to see her leave if it meant being rid of me.

With a nod to him, Mona followed me down the stairs to the patrol car. She settled herself comfortably on the passenger seat, leaning back against the door, much as she had on Effield's sofa.

Over the crackle of the radio, she asked, "Have you found out what happened to Anne?"

"No, but it doesn't look good." I asked if Anne had had enemies or particular friends.

"She wouldn't tell me. We weren't close. We just worked together." She paused. "What's with the client, McIvor?"

"She seems to be missing too. At least she's not at the address listed in her file. Alec Effield thinks she, and eleven, possibly sixteen, other clients moved and Anne just hadn't gotten around to recording the new addresses."

Mona sat, watching my hand on the steering wheel. "I doubt it."

"What?"

"Anne's hardly perfect, but inefficiency is not one of her faults. If you want to know about inefficiency, ask me; my caseload's always behind. But Anne—if a client moved this morning, Anne would have the address change on the computer by noon."

"Alec didn't seem to think so."

Mona said nothing. I wished I knew more about the welfare system; I didn't know enough to realize what I should ask. Mona seemed straightforward. She seemed like someone who would find subterfuge too great an effort.

"Was Alec involved with Anne?" I asked. "I mean, before you and he got together."

Mona smiled, pulling her feet up under her. "Don't worry. There's nothing between us."

"Nothing? I didn't pick that up from Alec."

"Well, what can I tell you? I think it's fair to say that he and I have different goals. I find him pleasant now and then, but I'm certainly not attracted to him. He, well, he'd love to go to bed with me, and he'd be appalled, no, disgusted, to see me in his apartment in the morning."

I sneaked a glance at Mona's face. There was no sign of hurt or anger, just the vague amusement that had characterized her during much of the discussion. I was finding I liked Mona Liebowitz.

"What about Anne, then?" I asked.

"You mean Alec and Anne? I don't know."

"Do you think it was likely?"

It was a moment before Mona answered. "I really don't know. Have you seen Anne?"

"No."

"Well, the easiest way for you to picture her is to think of the opposite of me." There was laughter in her voice.

I laughed too. That was the type of person I could picture with Alec Effield.

We were out of the hills by now. I turned the car left onto Grove. It would have been easy to lapse into a friendly conversation with Mona. To compensate, I questioned her answers more critically. Choosing my words, I said, "Anne may have been involved in some shady dealings with clients. Do you think Alec could have gotten her into them?"

"Alec couldn't lead an old lady across the street."

"But he is the supervisor."

Mona put a hand on my arm. "You can't be as innocent as you sound. Look, civil service is run by your old-time male chauvinist pigs and when they see one of their own little piggies coming along, they give him a pull. Anyone in our unit is more competent to supervise. Alec has the job for only one reason: because he has balls. And I don't mean that in the abstract."

"So Anne may have dreamed up whatever's going on and carried it out on her own?"

"Could be." Mona sat up straight. "Anne's more likely to have done things alone, not necessarily by choice—" She paused as if considering the wisdom of continuing.

"Not by choice?"

Mona took a breath. "Okay. Anne's a cheat. It's her nature, like having brown eyes. You learn that after you've been involved with her. She does it on everything. If she's going to split the gas on a trip she gives you less than half. She'll leave a dime tip and push it together with your quarter. I doubt she even realizes it."

But, I thought, someone may have realized it and had enough of Anne.

As I stopped the car by the address Mona had indicated, not more than three blocks from my own apartment, I noticed her looking at me, assessing my expression.

"You know," she said slowly, "it might be that I could find out things you can't. Maybe we could get together again."

Was this curiosity or self-protection?

Whatever Mona's motivation, I needed all the help I could get. I'd deal with the implications later. "I'll come by tomorrow evening."

"Good." Mona got out and shuffled up the path, around the house to the back.

I sat, idly watching the palm fronds flutter in the fog. Mona, Alec, Fern Day: they were either lying, hiding something, or at best trying to get a scoop on the investigation. Each of their interpretations of Anne differed, but even Alec was willing to admit she wasn't above taking bribes. What else had Anne been doing? Ask Nat, Alec had said.

Alec Effield was right. It was time to find Nat, wherever he was.

Chapter

11

I stopped by a pay phone and dialed Nat. As the phone rang, my anger grew. Slamming it down on the eighth ring, I stood there for a second, then dialed again, this time Nat's friend, Owen McCauley. It had been over a year since I'd talked to him and I suspected from the hesitation in his speech that anything he'd heard of me in that time had not been flattering.

"It's business, Owen. And I have to see Nat now. You can tell him I pressured you."

He laughed uneasily. "Okay. I'll tell him you threatened to tow my car." He hesitated again. "I don't really know where Nat is, but if I had to make a guess, I'd say the library. There's a new book in Nat's field that's just out. It's about Maud Gonne, Yeats' great love. It's reference, so if Nat's reading it—and odds are he is—he's been waiting for the publication for a couple of months —he's doing it in the library."

"Thanks, Owen. Your car will still be there in the morning."

I drove to the University campus. The main library

was not too far from Sproul Plaza at Telegraph. I'd been
past it in the days when Nat and I had gone for walks on
campus. But the campus was arranged for foot traffic
and driving was labyrinthine; I made several wrong
turns before I came upon the building. I was glad that it
was something I normally had no call to do. The campus
police handled every crime there; the University of California force was one of the largest forces in the state.

For a Wednesday night in October—early in the term—
the library was quite full. After a whispered interchange
with the reference librarian I made my way through,
looking over a variety of heads. No Nat.

To the librarian, I said, "I understand you just got in a
new book on Maud Gonne."

"Not that I know of."

"Would you check? She was a friend of Yeats."

Her shrug was not accommodating, but she did check,
a procedure that consumed five minutes, and produced
from her a smug shake of the head.

"Nothing connected with Yeats? Well, what about Irish
poetry, or Noh plays, or theosophy?"

"Nothing."

"You sure?"

Another grudging shrug preceded her departure and it
was five minutes more before she returned to assure me,
in very crisp tones, that nothing related to any of those
topics had come in.

Damn! I should have known better than to trust Owen
McCauley.

Back in the car, headed toward the station, I was considering what kind of cop couldn't even find her own ex-
husband, when I came to Shattuck Avenue. Abruptly, I
turned south toward the city library. Owen hadn't speci-
fied which library. Muttering an apology to the thought
of Owen, I stopped.

I left the car in a loading zone, hurried up the library
steps and turned left to the reserve room. Nat was sitting
at a table by the far wall, his head suspended above a
book, his hair hanging over his eyebrows. He must have

been there a while. I glanced at the book. It looked about two hundred pages and he was not half through. He'd probably come directly from the welfare department meeting in Oakland—a half hour drive at most. It was almost seven o'clock now.

Sliding into the seat next to him, I said, "Nat."

He glanced over, half smiled, then a look of confusion came over his face. "What are you doing here?"

"I have to talk to you about Anne."

"Anne? Oh, Anne. What did you find out?"

I suggested someplace more private, and followed Nat toward the stacks. As we climbed the stairs, I noticed the title of his book—*The Life of Major John MacBride*— MacBride, the "drunken, vainglorious lout" of "Easter 1916," the man Maud Gonne married after repeatedly refusing Yeats.

"Nat," I said, swallowing hard, "what happened at Anne's apartment Monday night?"

Nat stopped by a row of volumes on rock gardens. "What?"

"Nat, you left your pen there—the pewter pen your father gave you. It was in Anne's apartment."

Nat's hand went to his shirt pocket, then to his pants. He didn't look at me. "Oh, the pen. Anne borrowed it."

I said nothing. Nat was particular about his possessions. The pen had been a birthday gift. I couldn't imagine his lending it to anyone, even someone special.

"Just before I dropped her off, she borrowed it. She said she was going to write a letter. She'd left her pen at the office."

"She didn't have another one at home? Come on, Nat."

"If you're going to take that tone, there's no point in discussing it. You're always on the offensive." He leaned back against the stacks, resting an elbow on the shelf.

"Nat, this isn't a personal argument. Something happened to Anne. Her apartment was a shambles. Furniture was overturned. There was blood on the walls. And we found clothes monogrammed "AMS" in a heap by the

Bay. It looks like Anne is dead. Now, what happened when you were there?"

Nat stared, the skin pulled tight across the bridge of his nose. "Dead. It's really hard to believe."

I put a hand on his arm. "What happened?"

"I don't know. I have never been in Anne's apartment. How would I know?"

"You never lend that pen."

"Well, I did this time."

I pulled my hand back. "Nat, this is not just a discussion between us. The fact that that pen was found in Anne's living room is in my report. If you're not being honest about this it will come out."

"You mentioned my pen?"

I said nothing.

"You talk about this being impersonal—nothing to do with our having been married—but it is personal. No one else would have connected that pen to me."

He was right, of course. "Nat, you called *me*. You could have just called the station, but we've been through all that. Tell me about leaving the pen."

"I did." The skin on his face seemed tauter yet.

I waited, knowing it was hopeless to expect him to add anything else. "Very well, then. Where were you on Monday night?"

"Monday? Monday?"

I watched him as he considered, trying to view him with the objectivity I would any witness. But it was impossible. I'd seen that look as he created excuses, as he avoided answers, as a prelude to telling me I wouldn't understand. I glanced away, deciding to focus solely on his statements.

"Monday, Nat."

"Ah, yes. Monday was Alec Effield's little party. He—"

"He had a *party* Monday night?" That certainly wasn't the impression I'd gotten from him or from Mona. I tried to reconstruct their statements. Had either one said anything to suggest they'd been alone, or could they have been as easily referring to a small party?

"Go on," I said.

Nat half raised an eyebrow, another gesture I'd seen often in situations he found tiresome. "Every so often Alec has these little get-togethers for his workers at his place. He seems to feel he should. It's basically an ill-conceived idea, since not many of us can tolerate each other and usually a few drinks only serve to bare the hostilities."

"Were all the workers there?"

"Oh, yes. Every last one, except Jeremy Dales and the clerk, who, thank God, are on vacation. So what we were left with was Alec, Mona, Fern, Anne, and me. Still an unpleasing grouping."

Strange that Fern hadn't mentioned that party when I asked her about Monday; it was an easy alibi. "Were you there all evening, all of you?"

Nat sighed, and I tried to ignore the implicit condescension. "I don't know how long the rest of them stood it, but Anne and I left at eight-thirty. And then—I know you'll ask—I drove Anne to a supermarket on Shattuck. And then I dropped her off at her apartment. I did not go in."

"And?"

"I went home."

"Directly?"

"Yes."

"Did you see anyone?"

"No."

"Maybe someone saw you?"

"I doubt it."

"Then there's no proof, Nat. You could as easily—"

"I did talk to Owen on the phone, as soon as I got home."

I looked up. Maybe Nat's story was true. If he'd left Effield's at eight-thirty and done what he said, he couldn't have gotten home before nine thirty-five, maybe nine forty. "What time was the call?"

"Twenty to ten, maybe quarter of."

"Of course, that's still not proof. You could have called

him from anywhere. You could even have used Anne's phone."

Nat squeezed the book around the pencil that marked his place; the cover strained to an ellipse. "Jill, Owen called me. Does that satisfy your requirements?"

"On that. For now." I put up a hand to forestall his rebuttal. "You asked me to check this. I've spent a day and a half on it and I'll be spending more time. I've got other cases that are gathering dust. The least you can do is answer my questions civilly."

Nat's face barely changed; it simply solidified from a face to a mask.

I took a deep, calming breath and said, "Nat, there was something going on with Anne's cases. What do you know?"

"Does that connect with Anne's being dead?"

"Other than your pen, it's the only lead in the case. Do you understand? Nat, your pen was there, for whatever reason. You worked closely with Anne. You were the last person to see her . . . alive. Don't you see how that looks?"

"But, Jill, you know that I would never—"

"I can't tell Lieutenant Davis that you are my former husband and you wouldn't kill anyone. I need something concrete, Nat." I pulled out my pad and opened it to the list of case names. "Do these mean anything to you?"

He glanced down the page. "No. Who are they?"

"Anne's cases." I explained about the addresses.

"Anne helped me on my cases; I didn't work on hers."

"You knew Anne. There was something going on with these cases. Anne took bribes from her clients. What do you think—"

"I can't believe that. Anne wouldn't—"

"It's true."

"She wasn't like that."

"Then what was she like?"

Nat bit down on his lip. "It's hard to say. She's not quite what she seems."

"You'll have to be more explicit. I don't even know how she seems, much less how inaccurate that is."

He ran his teeth over his lower lip. "It's hard to describe. Let me think about it for a while." He started to turn, then said, "I'll tell you this, though. Anne was someone other women couldn't take."

I said nothing.

"Mona grilled me about her, too: What did she do with her time? Whom did she see? Did I think there was something going on between her and Alec? Or even Donn Day?" Nat shook his head. "That kind of bitchiness isn't like Mona. She never gets like that about anyone else."

I still said nothing.

"Maybe it's just working there—I mean, maybe it's the case distribution. Mona was having it out with Anne and Alec last week."

"About the cases?"

"I don't know. It was in Alec's office. I was at my desk trying to do some work."

"Why do you think Mona was so interested in Anne?"

Nat sighed. "I just told you, Jill. Anne's not a woman's woman. That's as clear as I can make it."

I knew from experience there was no sense in pressing him. Exasperated, I said, "Nat, you must have considered what happened to Anne."

"I've been very busy."

Without comment, I turned and walked down the stairs. Nat's concern for Anne certainly had been short-lived. Still, I knew Nat too well to doubt that he might have gotten so involved in his book that he had forgotten Anne.

Or did I know him? Did I merely know the Nat of a year or so ago? I'd changed in that time; why should I assume he'd remained static? Could he have been a partner to the bribes? Could he have called me because he needed to find Anne? I found it hard to believe.

But I wouldn't be able to explain that to Lt. Davis.

Chapter

When I banged on the glass door, Lt. Davis was in the process of straightening up his desk. He was a fastidious person. His forte was organization. And it had served him well in the Department. He had entered at the right time, in three years—the minimum—made senior patrol officer, and six months later, sergeant. Again in minimum time, he'd become a lieutenant and there he'd stayed, waiting for the captain's slot to become vacant. But the other two Watch commanders also had ambitions for the captain's job. They eyed each other, hoping for a false move, and they eyed Lt. Davis, aware that having a black captain with a master's degree would be almost more than Berkeley could resist.

Lt. Davis was alert, watching for flaws in his work—and ours.

He looked up as I opened the door.

"It's about time you reported in, Smith. You've left your beat low all evening."

"Sorry. It couldn't be helped."

"That's my decision, Smith. That's why there are Watch commanders."

"Yessir." I sat down on one of the hard wooden chairs that might as well have been a stool—I'd never seen anyone feel comfortable enough to lean against its back. "I've been following up a Missing Person's report."

"A report made by your ex-husband, directly to you."

"Yessir. I—"

"I'll transfer it to . . ." He tapped a caramel-colored finger against the desk.

"Lieutenant, hear me out first. I know this is rather unorthodox, but I have spent a day and a half on the case, and I think it's cost-efficient for me to complete it." I was walking a thin line here. Cost-cutting was in vogue nationwide these days, and our department, like all others, had felt the squeeze. But while it had only been fashionable recently in government, with Lt. Davis it was a way of life. Still, as much as savings would appeal to him, my attempt at making yet a second supervisory decision would not. I waited to see how well I'd balanced.

"Go on, Smith."

I explained about Nat's report, and the search of Anne's apartment. "There was blood on the wall. The lab crew sent in the specimens and the fingerprints, but—"

"I know. Three days at best."

"Still, the combination of a bloody apartment, an abandoned purse, and those monogrammed clothes that were turned in suggests more than just a standard missing person."

The lieutenant nodded. "What have you found on her?"

"Well, she was clearly more appealing to men than women. And not at all appealing to welfare clients. Beyond that, the most definite things people said were that she didn't talk about her private life, but she had come here two years ago. Effield, the welfare supervisor, knew her before. And the word among welfare clients is that she's on the take."

The lieutenant sat back, eyes half closed. I felt like I

was feeding data into a computer and when I had finished the input the machine would print out the correct answer.

"The interesting thing," I said, "is that no one at the welfare office, even Effield, who said he recommended Anne for the job, was surprised. Effield seemed distressed that it could be going on under his nose, but Mona Liebowitz took the news in stride."

"So?"

"Well, Anne had seventeen cases separated out. I can't come up with a good reason why. Effield said they might be waiting for address changes."

"Could be. Welfare clients move much more frequently than the average. These clients, were they heads of families or single adults?"

"Both. Twelve adults—all women—and five families. So far I've checked on four of the adults."

"Good. Deal with the adults first. Facts get muddled in families. The adults will save time."

I was tempted to add that some of the adults I'd run into—Delehanty in the forefront—were pretty muddled. "The intriguing thing is that of the four women who were listed as living in the Ranier Hotel off Telegraph, not one of them is there now and a long-term tenant claims none of them ever did live there."

"And this Effield says they moved?"

"He says probably. He's cagey. He put up a fuss about breaking confidentiality, but finally agreed to let me talk with one of the twelve, the one of my choice."

"So, Smith . . ." He sat, stroking his moustache. "So what do you make of all this?"

"These clients were paying off Anne Spaulding."

"Because?"

"They were breaking the rules. Excess income. It'd have to be excess income to make it worth her while. General Assistance clients only get two hundred a month. If that were their total income there wouldn't be much for Anne to go after. So they must have unreported income, enough to bribe her."

His eyes half closed again; his hand went back to the moustache. "It hardly seems worthwhile bribing a worker to keep getting two hundred a month."

"They also get food stamps and MediCal."

He nodded. "And a good cover for any illicit income."

I waited while he added this input.

"So you are assuming that one of these clients attacked her and then disposed of her corpse and clothes?"

"Tentatively." I had gotten caught before, agreeing too wholeheartedly. Don't develop theories too soon, the lieutenant had said, they box you in. "It all seems rather penny-ante for murder, but—"

"Nothing's too small to kill over." There was an unfamiliar note of weariness in his voice. "Check with Sex Crimes, Smith. See if these ladies are theirs." He paused again, as if awaiting the final printout. "I would like to take you off this case. There's no way you can avoid being too close, divorced or not. No matter how a marriage ends, your emotions don't shift back to neutral."

"I've got a statement from Nat, my ex-husband."

The lieutenant shrugged, discounting that.

I leaned forward, aware that the blood was coming to my face. I wished I had a fine brown skin like his, one that didn't flush so obviously. "If you're not sure, send someone to check his alibi."

He rubbed the wiry hairs of his moustache.

"It'll save manpower."

I waited. Why was I so anxious to hang onto this case? I hadn't mentioned the pewter pen. Although Lt. Davis had read about it in my report, he would have no way of knowing the pen's value to Nat. Was I protecting Nat? I knew he was lying, but I didn't know why. Still, another officer wouldn't even realize that. No, my knowledge of Nat was an advantage here. And there was more than Nat involved now. I didn't want a case, any case, taken from me with a vote of no confidence. And, I wanted to know what had happened to Anne Spaulding. And, I wanted to find that out myself.

Still, I waited. There was no more to say.

"Smith," he said, putting out his words with care, "I am counting on your professional competence. I am assuming if you cannot be objective you will let me know immediately. You understand?"

"Yessir."

"Howard will check the alibi."

"Uh huh."

"You, of course, will say nothing."

"Yessir." I was surprised how automatic my agreement was.

"And Smith—"

"Yes."

"We could have Spaulding's body turn up any time. When that happens this case will be in Homicide. Keep on top of everything and have it ready to transfer."

Howard had been summoned as soon as I left the lieutenant's office. I dictated the reports of the day's interviews—ready for transfer. I left a request for Sex Crimes. I summarized the case so far. It was twenty to eleven.

I didn't know what I'd gained by that interview with the lieutenant—perhaps another day or so before he transferred the case, not to a friend like Howard or Pereira, but to a detective in Homicide. The case would be gone, and even when solved, I would never know the little details of it. A detective wouldn't come by and tell me why Fern Day lied about the party or what motivated Mona Liebowitz. The only point he'd discuss with me would be the pewter pen.

I could feel my neck tense as I thought of the pen, of Nat.

There was some paperwork I could do till eleven, statistics to be compiled from my cases. There was always paperwork waiting to be done. There had been paperwork piling up, waiting for me, when I took this job.

"Great thoughts?"

I looked up. "Connie. I didn't hear you come in."

"It's not exactly silent in here, but I didn't tiptoe in. You just looked so caught up staring at that form, I wondered if you'd found something in it that had eluded me."

She settled atop the desk behind me.

"No. What I was doing was not so much thinking as trying to avoid it."

"Nat, huh?"

"Yes," I said, embarrassed. How many times had I carried on about him? "But not in exactly the traditional sense."

"Nat in a new arena of conflict?" A grin flashed on and off her face.

I hesitated.

"Nat in the Anne Spaulding case, perhaps?"

"Right. You recall his pen in Anne's living room?"

Connie nodded.

"Well, Nat claims he was never in her apartment. He says he lent her the pen. I may know very little of Nat now; I may never have known as much as I thought I did; but I do know how incredibly fussy he is about those possessions that are important to him. He does not lend those things. One time I took a piece of his engraved stationery—Nathaniel Hawthorne Smith—because I was completely out of writing paper and I had to get a letter off that night. I realized it was a mite presumptuous, but Nat was not just put out; he was angry. The paper was one of those things he didn't lend. The pen was another. His father gave it to him three years ago."

"So Nat didn't lend Anne the pen. Therefore the pen entered the house with Nat. And therefore Nat lied to you."

"Right. And my question to myself is why. And why did I take this case to begin with."

"You still care for him?" Connie suggested in a carefully neutral tone.

"No. I mean, I'm not furious with him any more. I feel some concern, some residual care for a person I lived with for four years; but it's not like I want to go back with him."

"But . . . ?"

"Well, I do feel somehow responsible. I mean, no one but me would realize Nat was lying about the pen, and no one else would understand that that was due to some peculiarity of his, not to a guilty secret. So if I were to transfer the case now, I would put Nat in a rather awkward position."

"One which he could deal with by telling the truth."

"But he wouldn't. He'd get huffy and obnoxious and probably push the officer who interviewed him into arresting him because he made himself look so suspicious."

Connie stood up. "Jill, this is a grown man. One who initiated this case. Why are you viewing him like a six-year-old?"

Without thinking, I said, "Because I left him. Because my life is going fine and he had to give up the one thing that mattered to him."

Connie said nothing. I stared blankly, stunned by my realization. It was a while before I said, "Thanks, Connie."

"Are you going to transfer the case, then?" she asked.

"Oh, no. Now that I can see what I've been doing, it's a lot clearer how to handle this. I'm not going to imperil the investigation for Nat. And, frankly, because of all that I know about Nat, and what little he said about the people he worked with, I can conduct this investigation better than someone else."

"Okay." Connie sounded unconvinced.

"Good night." It was a few minutes after eleven. The room was abuzz with the changing shifts. The noise had to have been going on for ten minutes, but I hadn't noticed. Now I realized that Williams, my counterpart on the Morning Watch, was at the end of the aisle, waiting for me to vacate the desk. Quickly I stacked the forms I'd been perusing when Connie'd come by, pushed my phone messages into a pile and paperclipped them before putting them in my drawer.

It was nearly quarter-after when I finally stood up. I was relieved not to see Howard, relieved that Connie

Pereira had already left. I had discussed the case enough.

I opened the door and stepped out into the fog. The parking lot was silent now. I made my way through the rows of cars, patrol cars waiting to be taken on beat, personal cars merely waiting. Apparently Morning Watch hadn't seen the memo prohibiting personal cars in the lot yet. My Volkswagen was across the street, under an elm tree. I was nearly abreast of it when I saw the old Asian man. He was sitting cross-legged atop the hood! He looked like one of the pictures on Sri Fallon's wall.

"What are you doing?" I demanded. "You're denting my hood."

"Ah, yes," he said, nodding. Straggly gray hair fell from a balding pate onto robed shoulders. His arms were crossed over an appallingly protruding abdomen. I was glad I hadn't left anything in the trunk beneath him.

"Get off there."

"Ah, yes." He nodded again.

Didn't he speak English? Was he a refugee? Despite his girth, he looked unwell. The lines in his yellowish face were deep. Even under the shadow of the elm it was apparent he was old and sick. Regardless, he couldn't spend the night on the hood of my car!

"I'll help you down," I said slowly.

The man laughed. His head rose; his face rejuvenated. He pulled off the gray wig and laughed louder. "I told you I'd see you. How about that drink?" It was Skip Weston from Theater on Wheels.

"Weston," I said, "you're quite an actor. I'm just relieved that stomach isn't real."

"I'll accept your accolades—that's what I'm in theater for—but they should be aimed not at my acting but my make-up."

"You had me going."

Weston tossed a pillow—the "stomach"—down onto the wheelchair on the far side of the car. "And this make-up job is almost entirely without putty or wax. Doing an

Oriental is a challenge. I wasn't sure I could convince you. You need the orangey-yellow pancake base, but there's a gray touch to the skin any amateur will miss. And, of course, the epicanthic fold to the eyes—no easy thing. It would have been much easier for me to be black or Indian, but I wanted to give you the *pièce de résistance.*"

"Very convincing." What was behind Weston's performance? He'd gone to a lot of trouble; was there more behind this than just the challenge of making me have a drink with him?

"I've spent a lot of time on make-up. It's especially important in a wheelchair theater where you don't have all the other possible differentiations between actors. See, appearance is what an audience deals with first. And even that doesn't have to be perfect. Once you give them the major clues, they fill in around them."

"Weston—"

"You saw an old yellow man here sitting cross-legged, and you assumed the rest. I didn't have to—"

"Weston, you're on my car."

"Look, it's like lying—"

"Weston—" But he talked through me. Make-up was obviously his passion and I decided it would be easier to wait him out and see if his monologue would reveal the motivation behind his presence here.

"See, if you sit next to a guy on a bus and he starts telling you the story of his life, you don't question it. Not so long as there's internal consistency. Well, that's how make-up is. It's a lie with internal consistency."

When he paused for breath, I said, "It *is* interesting, but I'm going to have to ask you to get down off my car."

"And then we'll go for a drink? All this has given me a great thirst."

When I hesitated, he added, "The bar I'm suggesting is Dalloway's in Oakland. It has, among its other attractions, a number of artists who know Donn Day. You were asking about him yesterday. Look on this as work, if that makes it acceptable, though I'd rather you considered it pleasure."

With Fern Day lying, I was going to have to deal with Donn and his Monday night whereabouts. "Okay. I'll meet you there in forty-five minutes. Obviously we both have to change."

As I watched him grab the aerial, plant his other hand on the hood, and swing himself down onto the chair, I couldn't help but be impressed by his gymnastic strength and agility.

The permanent impression of Skip Weston was, of course, on the hood of the car.

At home I dawdled in front of the closet, rejecting the idea of wearing my one skirt; regardless of what Weston might think about this meeting, for me it was business. Seeing anyone involved in the case had to be business; socializing could come only after the case was solved.

I looked wistfully toward my sleeping bag. It had been a long day already.

Putting on what could only be described as serviceable jeans and a sweater, I headed for the car. The streetlight bounced off the Weston dent. I got in, started the engine, and turned on the radio. There was only static—the Weston-bent aerial.

I turned the radio off and dedicated the time of my drive to contemplation of Fern Day. Why had she lied about the party at Effield's? It was a much better alibi than the one she'd given me—at home with her husband. As alibis, spouses were slightly better than pets. If Fern were not protecting herself, was she protecting Donn? Did she suspect Donn had been at Anne's apartment Monday night?

I pulled up in front of a plastic-fronted bar—Dalloway's.

Inside, the patrons were clumped into groups, one loudly discussing the merits of California sculptors, another complaining about the lack of standards in local art fairs. In the far corner sat Skip Weston.

In the time I'd changed from uniform to jeans and a sweater, Skip Weston had transformed himself from the ailing octogenarian back to a robust young man. His dark hair glistened and those ebon eyes shone, moving nervously from side to side, finally lighting on me. He smiled and his face relaxed. Had he suspected I wouldn't come?

He pulled out a chair and I sat down.

"Now is the moment of truth," he said. "What is the nature of this drink you've deigned to accept?"

"A beer," I said, matching the underlying defensiveness of his tone. "We cops drink beer."

"Two Henry's, Tom," he said and added to me, "I hope drinking from a glass instead of a bottle won't destroy your image?"

"I'll try to adjust."

When the drinks came the waiter settled down with them. In another moment two more men wandered over, greeting Skip Weston with enthusiasm.

For a while I sat back, listening to their discussion of various gallery shows. There was a quilt show on College Avenue that got high marks, and a pottery exhibit that was dismissed—fit only to eat off.

"And the Day show opens Friday," Skip said, with a wink at me.

"Donn Day?" I put in.

"Yeah, do you know him?" a blond man asked.

"Not really. I know of him. I saw one of his paintings this afternoon." I described the one over Fern's desk. "I understand it's not one of his better things."

"Few are," the waiter said.

"But he's having a show."

"Listen, honey, obviously you aren't familiar with the art world. Anyone can have a show if they know people. Isn't that right, Ted?"

The man called Ted nodded. "But ol' Donn's not so bad. I mean, his stuff isn't. If he were a normal guy instead of such an ass . . ."

"And if he didn't have that behemoth of a wife galumphing around him . . ."

They all laughed.

"But he does have a good sense of color." Skip said it, and I couldn't help but feel it was more an attempt to rescue a friend than a true statement of opinion.

"Do you know Donn well?" I asked Ted.

"I've known him since art school when he was Donald Dahlgren."

More laughter.

"Have you seen him recently?"

Ted put a hand on my arm. "Do I look like someone who would hang out with Donn Day?"

"Besides," the waiter said, saving the problem of how to reply, "if the striving Mr. Day is opening Friday, knowing him, he hasn't been out of the gallery for days. Jesse," he said to the third man, "do you remember when Day had three canvasses up at the University Museum and he spent two entire days bitching about the lighting?"

"Do I?" Jesse said. "By the time he finished, he'd raised such a commotion that the staff shifted the lights and left my work in the dark."

"Yeah, and yours sold!"

"A new marketing technique!" Skip added.

"You may have been missing a good thing with all those lights, Jesse," the waiter said. "Darkness may be your forte."

I laughed with the others. If I could have relaxed, it would have been pleasant here. But I wondered, as I leaned back, half listening to a conversation to which I couldn't have contributed if I'd wanted—why had Skip Weston insisted I come here? Why had he had his friends all but provide an alibi for Donn Day? And if Donn were occupied Monday, why had Fern lied?

As the hour drifted toward two A.M., the crowd thinned till only the waiter remained with us. When he got up to answer a call from another table, Skip Weston said to me, "Are you ready to go?"

I stood up. Weston had managed to talk to me only in the group, and now that that had dissipated, he was leaving. Strange.

I walked beside him to his van, and as he pulled the wheelchair in after, he said, "You might check Donn Day's studio."

"Why?"

"It might be interesting."

"Look, if you know something—"

"I don't *know* anything. It just could be interesting."

He started the engine and I let him go. I had the feeling that the face Skip Weston had shown me tonight was merely another false face, and I didn't know what was behind it.

Chapter

13

At eight-thirty on the dot Thursday morning I passed five empty desks on my way to Alec Effield's office in what had once been the kitchen. For one who depended on eight hours of sleep, last night had been a disaster; twice while driving to the office I had realized my eyes were closed. I was only grateful that Nat had not made it to work on time. The last thing I wanted was to deal with him, angry at being interrogated by Howard, and to have our relationship presented to Mona, Alec, and Fern Day in all the bitchiness of post-divorce.

I moved quickly into Effield's office. To one side of his desk lay the half-done copy of Suzanne Valadon's "After the Bath."

Glancing at the original sketch pinned on the bulletin board I nodded approvingly. "When it's done I doubt you could tell your copy from the print."

Effield looked away, embarrassed. "Thank you. I like to sketch. I'm afraid I'm not very original, but I do have a facility for reproducing. Unfortunately there's little call for that in the non-criminal world."

I smiled, surprised that Effield would have even that mildly humorous thought. But my silence seemed to unnerve him, as if he were still on the spot from having been complimented.

"It relaxes me, you see. It's very orderly, every line has its place. If you're careful, everything has to come out right, not like in the welfare department." Looking away, still awkward, he picked up a manila folder marked "Yvonne McIvor." "I hope this will allay your suspicions."

"I hope so." I sat down on a green chair. "Are you going to call her now?"

"Clients don't get up this early, usually."

"They do for the police."

Effield seemed loathe to press the point. Taking the easier alternative, he dialed the phone and held it out so I could hear it ringing. On the fifth signal a woman's voice said, "Hello." She didn't sound all that groggy to me. Perhaps Effield had been a supervisor too long to recall what time clients arose. He put the receiver back to his ear and I listened as he explained that he was cooperating with the police and Ms. McIvor's name had been chosen at random to check on quality control. She must have had some hesitation for Effield explained the whole thing again and then answered questions. It was fully five minutes before it was agreed that I would be at her house in half an hour.

Yvonne McIvor's apartment was the sole dwelling over a cluster of small shops set apart from rundown stucco houses half a mile west of Telegraph.

As I climbed the steep, dark stairs between two shops I wondered what kind of woman would brave such an isolated apartment. I must have been expecting an Amazon, for when she opened the door I was surprised to find Yvonne McIvor no taller than myself.

She was light-skinned for a black woman. As if to refute that lightness she wore a wide Afro and bright dashiki. And her apartment picked up the theme. It was a statement of racial pride, with African batiks on the walls, carved native figures on tables, and record covers featuring black artists displayed from three racks on a floor-to-ceiling pole. An old record player stood next to a battered television set, but it was from a portable radio that the soul music blared forth.

"You the cop?" the woman asked, turning down the radio.

I offered her my shield, but the uniform seemed to satisfy her. She motioned me to an old couch covered totally with a fringed rectangle of cloth.

"So what you want? These welfare dudes, they're always checkin' up on each other. They're so busy watchin' for rip-offs they got no time for nothin' else, you see what I mean? But you go 'head, honey, you tell me what you want now. See, 'cause I ain't gonna fuss. I'm just playin' the game, you understand?"

I nodded. "Ms. McIvor, where did you live before you moved here?" In contrast to McIvor, I sounded like a parody of "The Man."

" 'Fo here? Well, see, I just come here to Berkeley, so I stayed at this hotel. I don't have people to stay with, so I just stay there till I could find me a nice place." She lifted her chin, indicating the apartment.

"When did you move here?"

"Right on pay day."

"You mean as soon as you got your welfare check? The first?"

"Right." She leaned back, shoulders moving to the hard beat of the music.

"And your eligibility worker was Anne Spaulding?"

"Yeah. I hear she's gone," she said, elongating the last word. "That was one tight woman. Honey, she wouldn't give her own mother a break. If you didn't have everything, and I mean every little scrap of paper, in at the hour, you was gone. Off. Out in the cold with just your bare ass."

"When did you tell her you moved?"

"The first. I sent in the rent receipt."

The first had been Saturday, two days before Anne Spaulding disappeared. "How soon would she have recorded the change?"

Yvonne McIvor's brown eyes widened. She shrugged. "I don't know what *she* did. I only know *I* had to let her know right away. Like I say, Miz Spaulding don't take nothin' on trust."

"Your case file was separate from the others. Why?"

She shrugged again. "Dunno. Maybe 'cause I moved."

I took out the list of clients and read off the other eleven names. "Tell me about these women."

"I don't know them. A couple names I heard."

"Which ones?"

"Linda Faye, I heard that, and Janis Ul . . . um . . . Ul-something."

"Ulrick. Where do you know them from?"

"Honey, I don't know them. I just heard the names. I don't recall where from."

"At the hotel?"

"Maybe. See, I keeps to myself. I don't put my business on the street, and when I see someone else's there, I cross over."

I sat a moment, staring at the African batik behind Yvonne. I put the list away. "Anne Spaulding was taking bribes."

Yvonne stared, as if waiting for me to continue, then her eyebrows rose. "Listen, honey, you're not saying *I* paid her off? Shit. What'd I use to pay off with? You see? The welfare don't give me but two hundred dollars a month. This place here costs a hundred-eighty. Where you think this payoff is gonna come from?"

I waited. The beat from the radio sounded louder.

"Why should I pay her? What for? She wasn't doin' nothing for me, you hear?"

"But you know about the bribes, don't you?"

"No!" Her fist hit her thigh. "Like I said, I don't go stickin' my nose around. Look, when you come up in the ghetto and you stay in dives like that hotel, you learn to be deaf."

"Other people, other welfare clients, know. Does it surprise you?"

She sat forward. "Miz Spaulding, she could. Why not? She sure don't care about folks. Only thing is, you see, it's so small time. Miz Spaulding, she's a high flyer, and the little bit she could get off us—she wouldn't stoop down to pick it up."

"What about her other clients? What did they think of her?"

Yvonne sat back. She seemed to be considering her response. "I don't speak for other folks, you understand, but I guess everyone pretty much thought she was shit. Leastways, I never heard nothin' else. One old dude was carryin' on how he was goin' right up to her house and tell her."

"You know where she lived?"

"*I* don't, but this dude acted like he did. Like I say, I'm not lookin' for trouble, so if he say he knows"—she shrugged—"he knows."

"What's his name?"

She shrugged again. "Search me. He's just some old dude at the welfare."

"A client, you mean?"

"Honey, they ain't hardly got no dudes, young or old, workin' there."

"Let's get back to the old man, the client. When did you hear him threaten to go to Anne Spaulding's house?"

"Last week? Week before? Not long ago. He said she better get her act together 'cause he knew what she was and everyone else on the welfare knew and he wasn't going to put up with no cheat no more."

"He said all that in the welfare office?"

She laughed. "Looks like you don't spend much time there. Otherwise you'd know you hear people screamin' and yellin' and callin' their workers plenty worse than cheat."

"But he did call her a cheat, there?"

"Sure did." She hesitated. "I couldn't swear, you understand."

"I understand." Flipping a page in my pad, I said, "Is there anything else you can tell me about Anne Spaulding?"

Yvonne waited, but the pretense of thought didn't come across. "If she's gone, I ain't cryin'." She leaned over and turned the radio up.

As I walked down the steep stairway, I thought what a disappointment Yvonne McIvor had been. Was she lying? Did she know nothing? Or was I on a wild goose chase with these cases of Anne's?

I could have accused her of prostitution—could have seen what she'd say. But I'd decided to wait to hear from Sex Crimes. Yvonne McIvor would still be there.

Irritably, I got into the car and headed back toward the welfare office.

Chapter

14

Donn Day's studio was in the arts complex that included Theater on Wheels, about a mile west of Yvonne McIvor's apartment. I wanted to see it at a time when I wouldn't be likely to run into Skip Weston, and if Weston was half as tired as I was, he'd still be in bed now.

I peered through the picture window that ran the width of the studio. Donn Day was present only in photographic image. Doubtless the original was rearranging the lighting at the gallery for his upcoming show.

Had he been here I might have found out what, if anything, was going on between him and Anne, and where he had been on Monday night. Now I satisfied myself with focusing on his wall, half of which held canvasses similar to the one above Fern's desk. The other half of the wall, entitled "Donn Day at Work," sported photos of a small man with carefully styled brown hair. His artfully disheveled clothes were splattered with paint. The photographer's lights had been gentle, barely showing the deep squint lines around his eyes.

From what I had heard of Anne Spaulding, it was hard

to imagine her with this bantam of a man. It was harder yet to picture him with Fern Day.

Pulling myself away, I checked my watch. It was after eleven. I had promised Alec Effield I would check back with him after I saw Yvonne McIvor. If I went to the office now I could catch him before lunch and I could have another go at Fern Day.

In contrast to the empty room I had seen before, the Telegraph branch welfare office was crowded. In the alcove-cum-waiting room, children clambered amongst feet; men in jeans and women in secondhand beaded blouses sat staring toward the interview booths. In spite of the signs prohibiting it, the air was heavy with smoke.

As I came around the doorway, I could hear a commotion. Inside one of the cubicles that housed half a fireplace, the low rumble of Nat's voice interspersed with the muddled shouts of another man. The man's outburst seemed to be centered on the word "bitch." I moved closer, but proximity did nothing for clarity and I had just cleared the booth when the door burst open and a man in a white suit emerged, shaking his head.

"Sri Fallon," I said. "What are you doing here? I thought you worked at the Bank of America."

Inside the booth the argument continued, as if no one had left.

"I do. I took time off to come here with one of my followers, to try to help him contain his unfortunate temper. As you can see, or hear, I have failed."

Thinking that it was a good thing to have Nat using up his anger in an argument with someone else, I said to Fallon, "I'm sure nothing terrible will happen."

"Probably, but he told me he once attacked a social worker in Chicago. I don't know. He could have been exaggerating. Who knows what goes on in the Chicago welfare department?" Sri Fallon leaned against Nat's desk. "I guess I'll just wait."

In the booth Nat's voice rose. The group in the waiting room inhaled in unison, and I had the impression they had returned their attention from the spectacle of a Sri and a woman cop back to the more volatile entertainment in the booth.

Sri Fallon glanced around the room, his face devoid of the calm confidence it had beamed forth when I'd seen him on his own ground.

"Well," I said, "I'll just—"

"Who's that?" Fallon was staring past at Mona Liebowitz. She sat back, feet tucked into an open desk drawer, another T-shirt displaying the ample outlines of her breasts. "Does she work here?" His eyes were wide with amazement.

"They don't have dress codes any more. This isn't the bank."

"Oh, no, it's not that. It's that I've seen her before, at the bank. She was standing across from the bank just watching. I thought—well, I know this is going to sound silly—I thought she was casing the place."

"Maybe she has an account."

"No. I'd know. Hers is not a . . . a face you forget."

I glanced over at Mona's broad undistinguished features. Her face by itself was eminently forgettable. "Did she do anything then?"

"No. She just stood there watching. It happened twice —on the first of the month and a month after that."

"And the bank hasn't been robbed."

"No, it's just—"

A roar of indistinguishable words came from the booth. Fallon jumped up, pushed past me and grabbed the door. As he went in, I could make out a tangle of gray hair and a swath of brown jacket behind him, then his voice, loud but surprisingly calm. The other voice sounded again, but more quietly, then Fallon murmured something and Nat spoke. Now it seemed like a normal conversation.

I stood a moment, noting Fern Day's vacant desk and the cardboard sign above it: "Ill."

"What's the matter with Fern?" I asked Mona.

She half-smiled. "Mental-health day."

I wondered what had caused Fern's need for a day off. Filing that away for future consideration, I headed to Effield's office.

Effield looked up. "Have you seen Yvonne McIvor?"

"In the flesh."

"And you're satisfied?"

"I can't deny she was there."

"See," he said, his lips curving up in a weak smile, "you should have trusted me."

His smug passivity irritated me. "Police investigations can't count much on trust, Mr. Effield. For instance, you never told me you were involved with Anne Spaulding romantically."

His fingers rubbed against one another. He stared down at them. "Well, it wasn't really romantic. We were both from New York, Anne and I. We knew each other. When Anne came out I spent time with her. She didn't know other people."

"You were more than friends."

Effield fingered the cases, rubbing loose a gummed label. "In New York you couldn't even say we were friends. I asked her out once. She said no. I didn't ask again."

"You must have had some kind of relationship, some almost-friendship, if you asked her out."

"No. I asked her out to start a friendship. At first a lot of the men approached her. But she made it clear that the welfare department was a place she was working by necessity. It was beneath her. And she certainly wasn't going to attach herself to any man who had to work there."

"And then she came here . . . ?" When Effield didn't pick up my line of thought, I said, "But you were more than friends here, weren't you?"

He stared down at the crumpled case label. "Yes and no. We went to bed a few times, over a year ago, but it was no great romance. It was just easy. I never had any illusions that it would go on."

"But you would have liked it to?" I pressed.

"No. Maybe. I never considered the possibility. I still

worked at the welfare department. And Anne might have changed some since New York, but not that much."

I considered my next question.

But Effield seemed caught up in his explanation of Anne. "She wasn't someone you'd get into a relationship with anyway. She was never satisfied with one man, or one place, or one interest. She always had things going. She liked adventure and new things. She liked being admired, flirting." He paused, staring down at the crumpled sticker. "Anne wasn't a person you would get into a deep relationship with, not after you knew her."

Shoving over a manila folder, I settled on the desk. "Mr. Effield, you said Anne liked new places. Do you think instead of being killed, she just left?" As soon as the words were out I felt ridiculous. Was I asking if Anne had left nude, after cutting herself up to bloody her clothes?

But Effield responded to the question. "No." His tone was definite. "Anne wasn't irresponsible. She would never have left without notifying us. She would have notified me." He paused; he seemed to be biting his cheek, holding in his emotions. "We weren't lovers, but I am sorry Anne's dead. No, don't ask me how I know. I just feel it."

"Then surely you want to help me. Something was going on in these cases. If you'd go through them with me—"

"No!" His eyes opened, as if he were startled by his own assertiveness. "I'm sorry. I have work to finish. It's almost noon." He headed toward the dining room door.

"Fine." I didn't move.

Effield stopped. He opened his mouth, said nothing. He'd exhausted his assertiveness. After a moment, he nodded and left.

As soon as the door closed, I opened the folders he'd shut—Anne's twelve cases. In each of them was a memo on NCR paper indicating the new address. The handwriting looked like Anne Spaulding's. All three copies of the NCR paper were still in each folder. Apparently welfare workers wasted the NCR paper just as we did, using it not only to make carbonless copies, but just for notes.

How had I missed these before? All I recalled were the four legal-sized sheets in each case. I had been in a hurry. I didn't know what I was looking for. Still, it was careless. It unnerved me.

I could hear Effield's voice in the next room. There was no time to contemplate. I copied the addresses and was just closing the last folder when Effield returned.

"Officer, what are you doing? You know that's against the law!"

Ignoring that, I said, "Where were these notes"—I held out a piece of NCR paper—"on Wednesday?"

"On Anne's desk."

"No. I checked that. They weren't in the case folders either."

"You looked at them before? Really, I must protest."

"Where were they?"

"I must ask you to leave."

"Mr. Effield, what's going on with these cases?"

Effield swallowed, turned, and walked back through the dining room door.

I knew he was lying. He wasn't likely to come back for a while. I could check through his desk, but I didn't know what I was looking for. Again, I wished I had a better knowledge of the welfare system.

I'd have to go at it from the other end—from my own turf—Telegraph Avenue.

Chapter

I had caught Lt. Davis before the meeting, told him I needed to see Donn Day, Fern Day, and Mona Liebowitz, and to check the new addresses for Anne's clients. I could skip staff meeting, I suggested. But the lieutenant was not having that. Send Pereira, he said. I, as a beat officer, needed the information he was about to disseminate. Cost-effective, he added. I could see my argument of the previous night had not been so subtle as I'd thought.

So I sat in staff meeting listening to the lieutenant's summary of his meeting with the mayor, to the animal control officer's semi-annual plea for more help from us. I glanced at the hot-car list, at the list of things Night Watch wanted us to watch for. And I thought of Pereira banging on door after door asking for Anne Spaulding's eleven remaining clients. There were worse things than staff meetings.

And afterwards I waited at my desk for Howard to show up and for Pereira to come back from Donn Day's gallery. I sorted through my IN box, glancing at memos and tossing them out. Fern Day had been in and identified Anne's clothes. I filed that report, and sent in a request to be notified about any unclaimed female bodies recovered from San Francisco Bay or found in surrounding county morgues. Halfway through the box, I came on the lab report; back in two days—not bad.

From the blood samples taken in Anne's apartment, the lab had found two types—A positive and O positive. The blood on the clothes was A positive, and the two subgroups matched. So I could assume that one person's blood—Anne's—had stained both the dress and the apartment walls.

But the fingerprint report, the one that might have provided a lead, was a bust. The only clear prints in the apartment formed one set—doubtless Anne's. There were smudges on the lamp, but only one whole print, a thumb, and it belonged to the set. Nat's pen produced nothing telling—it was too slender to have captured a full print and even the partials were blurred.

I filed the reports and looked through the rest of the material in the IN box, and was just getting ready to dictate a note about Sri Fallon's mention of having observed Mona Liebowitz at the bank, when Howard walked up.

"Pretty elusive ex-husband you have. Not at work, not at home."

"It took you this long to track him down! Where'd the other workers say he was?"

"They didn't. No one was there. I was tied up with the lieutenant, and by the time I got there they were closed." He sat on my desk, pushing papers out of the way with his hand.

"What were you with the lieutenant for?"

"My thief, and the ever-diminishing supply of auto parts. Lieutenant Davis read me a list of everything that's been stolen, with prices. What do you think that guy's been doing with my stuff?"

"Maybe he's building his own police car, bit by bit, in the basement."

"Starting with the outside?"

"You don't need an engine in the basement."

Howard nodded. "Maybe so. Whatever, this is my last day. The lieutenant is fed up with the pettiness and with me. No thief, no car. If I don't get him today, I'm on station duty indefinitely."

"We'll get him. What's the plan?"

"Same as before. This time ending off the Avenue. I think—"

"Jill." It was Pereira, hurrying down the aisle, her hair still in disarray from the wind outside. "I've been to the Day show, and it was quite some show."

"Good," Howard said, "I'm ready for some amusement."

"Well, settle in, then." Pereira could barely control her grin. Planting herself on the desk across the aisle, she said, "After a lengthy prologue about himself—rising artist, widely known, with growing following and invitations to teach—he offered me a glass of wine and his body."

"Seriously?" I asked.

"Yes, indeed. It wasn't quite that blunt, but it wasn't done with velvet gloves either. I got the feeling," she said, again controlling her expression with difficulty, "that he didn't want to be too explicit for fear of being accused of offering a bribe."

When the laughter stopped, I said, "Mr. Day's sense of aesthetic evaluation must stop when he looks in the mirror."

Howard put out a hand. "Let's get to the serious stuff. Did you take him up on it?"

"I told him I'd consider it later."

I laughed again, then felt a rush of pity, thinking of Fern Day. Was she ignorant of her husband's profligate tendencies? Or did she choose not to see? Without Donn, Fern would be a priest without a church. I asked Pereira, "What did Donn say about the other night?"

"He was at the gallery till after midnight. I checked

with the workmen. He kept them there, too. They were only too glad to tell me."

"And he was never out of their sight?"

"Never went as far as the bathroom, and that's a quote." Pereira pushed herself up. "I'd like to tell you all the lurid details of the proposition, but I have eleven wandering welfare clients awaiting."

"You sound like 'The Twelve Days of Christmas,'" Howard said.

"By the time I finish they'll probably be singing that. Wait till I get a beat and can dispatch some peon to do the shitwork." She sauntered down the aisle, blond hair glistening in the afternoon sun.

Howard watched her go, then turned to me. "About the stake-out . . ."

"Yes?"

"Dusk?"

"Sounds good." I looked at his drawn, freckled face. "We'll get him this time, Howard."

"We better." He picked up his hat and headed for the stairs.

Checking the phone book, I dialed Fern Day's home number. But if she was too sick to work, she was not sufficiently incapacitated to be housebound. After eight rings I replaced the receiver.

I dictated my morning's interviews and checked out Anne's clothing—dress, bra, pants, and a half slip. The blood had spotted the dress, concentrated on the shoulder and chest areas. I was still wondering about the clothes and about Fern's phony alibi as I drove home, changed into jeans, and headed to Telegraph.

I got a large mug of *café latte*—it might have to last a while—and grabbed a seat by the front window of the Faded Rose Cafe just as Howard got out of his car and sauntered toward the Avenue. If he had followed our plan, he'd made his presence obvious, driving down Telegraph, double parking to get out and stretch his long legs, leaving the patrol car in front of the Faded Rose. Choosing the Faded Rose was a gamble. It was a spot that any Avenue regular passed ten times a day—half a block east of Telegraph, a block west of the University Museum, a block south of campus. Small specialty shops clustered around it, and the sidewalk in front was never empty. Odds were, the thief would bite, but the odds were also very good in favor of the thief's disappearing into the crowd or the shops.

Had the thief spotted Howard, he might well be in here now, waiting.

I glanced around the room. The group at the table next to me was watching the car. Across the room a man sat alone, staring out the window. Making a show of opening the newspaper, I observed him. He was small, long haired, with that loose body that could be mistaken for a woman's at a distance. And his clothes—old jeans and a flannel shirt—were the type the thief had worn.

Taking my eyes from him, I glanced at the trio next to me—two men and a woman. She wore a long cotton skirt and I dismissed her—too clumsy for a getaway. But either man could be the one. Their dress and appearances approximated the lone man across the room. Concentrating, I made out their conversation. They were speculating about tires—Howard's tires? Radials? Steel belted? Glass belted?

Still listening, I glanced back at the solitary figure, then at the patrol car and at the alley across the street. The thief could be there, or in another shop, or around the corner on Telegraph. Or he could not be here at all.

"Officer Smith?"

"What?" I looked up. If the thief was listening it was too late now. "Sri Fallon, we seem to be running into each other a lot."

"Ah, yes. I almost didn't recognize you in civilian clothes." He indicated a seat and when I nodded, sat down.

I shifted my chair so that I could stare past him out the window. Leaning forward, I glanced at the man across the room. If he was surprised by Sri Fallon's announcement of my title, he wasn't letting on. At the next table, conversations had stopped.

I tried to recall a picture of the thief as he'd outrun me Tuesday night—he was short, thin, fast, with long curly hair that could have been a wig. He could as easily have been short haired or bald. I remembered what Skip Weston had said about the effectiveness of make-up. The thief could even have been Sri Fallon.

"Is this your day off?" Sri Fallon asked.

"Huh? Oh, no. I'm on my dinner break."

"And you're only having coffee."

"I had a big lunch," I said, wondering how elaborate a story I was going to have to concoct. Outside, groups of students and street people strolled up Durant Avenue past Howard's car. The night was warm, the sun falling low toward the Pacific. Shadows hung from Howard's car.

". . . unearthed some facts?"

"What?" I jerked my head toward Sri Fallon.

"I was asking if you'd found anything on my neighbor." His face was calm, with no tight look or irritation at my ignoring him. It was as if the question had been asked by a third party.

"I've been checking into it, but I really haven't found anything."

"Do you think she's dead?"

"Why do you ask?"

He grinned. "I feel like I should say in a suspicious voice, 'Because I killed her and I want to know what you know.' Actually, it's because one of my devotees told me that she was disliked around here. When someone with that reputation disappears, death is always a possibility."

"Who was this devotee?"

"I wouldn't want to cause him any trouble."

"Unless he's done something you won't."

Fallon patted my arm. "I can't help but believe that's stretching the truth. Surely you'll admit that innocent observers, when they aren't pillars of Berkeley society, can be hassled."

The man across the room headed for the door. Un-crossing my legs, I watched him go out, down the steps, and onto the streets.

"You're giving it a lot of thought. Aren't you supposed to discuss that type of thing?" Fallon's tone was amused.

The man glanced at Howard's car, his eyes resting on the grill. If he decided on something as complicated as that I could have him while he was assembling his tools.

"Yes," I said to Sri Fallon, no longer remembering his question. The man glanced through the window, turned, and headed up the street.

"Are you waiting for someone?" Fallon asked.

"What? Yes. I don't know if he's really coming." I took a sip of cold coffee.

"Who is it? I don't mean to be nosy, but I do know most of the people around here. Between chanting and the Bank of America, you really get a cross section."

"Surely people bank elsewhere, too." A pair of Hare Krishnas, heads shaven, orange robes blowing in the evening breeze, stopped by the car, blocking my view. I pushed the chair to the right.

When I settled, Fallon said, "No. Almost everyone here uses my branch. Not only because of me." He grinned—it was the same puckish expression he'd had when com-menting on Anne Spaulding's sun-drenched, nude body. "It's just that it's the most convenient bank—not in the sense of location—it's the one off Telegraph—but it's fast and has parking. Anne Spaulding used it for a while, a year ago. She didn't recognize me, of course." He fin-gered the lapel of his white suit. "Lots of people who work around here come in. So, to get back to my point, finally, I may have seen your friend."

The Hare Krishnas moved closer to the car, looking through the window. I braced to move, waited, said to Fallon, "Not likely." The Krishnas stayed put. "Sorry. I'm really distracted. I'm having personal problems, and I guess they're clouding my mind."

"If you'd like to talk about them—"

"No. . . . Thanks, though."

"No, really, I don't pretend to any esoteric knowledge and I won't ask you to do three Hail Marys in chant, but I am a rather good listener."

I started to protest, eyes still on the stationary Krishnas, but Fallon continued. "You know where I am. If you feel like it, drop by."

"Thanks." The Krishnas were conferring, moving back from the car, glancing about. "Your follower—the one who mentioned Anne—I'm going to have to know his name."

"You never answered my question, you know—the one about hassling."

The Krishnas moved off slowly, still looking back. I let my tensed legs relax, and spread my fingers apart and rested them on the table. "Hassling? Well, all I can tell you is that I'll be fair. It's information I want, and it's usually easiest to get if you're straight with a person."

The shadows deepened. On the far side of the patrol car I thought I spotted a head at door level. Stretching up in my chair, I could make out a shoulder and hands.

The hands were on the rear-view mirror.

I muttered something to Sri Fallon and hurried to the door, outside, and down the steps.

The thief looked up, started, and took off up the street, away from Telegraph, shirttail flailing, sneakers splatting on the sidewalk. The long curly hair flowed back at me as I ran after, swerving around groups of strollers.

The thief passed the Ice Cream Shop, just as four cone-carriers emerged. Ignoring their cries of outrage, I pushed between them. The thief was half a block ahead. I was gaining. He crossed the street, darting in front of a pick-up.

I cut in behind a motorcycle, yelling, "Stop! Police!"

He kept moving, east across Bowditch. Howard would be waiting on Bowditch one block south. The thief glanced to the right and then left. He stopped, momentarily. He'd seen Howard. Would he cut north now? I could lose him that way.

Pressing my legs faster, I crossed the street just as he

turned left into the gates of the University Museum.
Pushing harder, I came up to the arch and stopped, panting. Would Howard realize he was in here, or would he
go on?

I stared into the courtyard. No one was visible.

The courtyard was akin to a cement shoebox, with the
east side formed by the darkened glass of the museum
itself and the south end, where I stood, open only at the
gate. It was dusky now and deep shadows hung off the
west wall and the high cement divider that bisected the
box halfway across, west to east. The grass rose in tiers
to the west, and northward it climbed to a grassy mound
next to the divider, then continued upward in steps to
the exterior wall. Behind the divider, I knew, was a set of
descending tiers, leading downward to a pair of cement
benches by the base of the west wall.

Two yards ahead of me by the museum gate was a
sculpture—a four-foot metal ball with a hole in the center. He could be behind that. To my left halfway to the
divider was another metal sculpture. There were a hundred places to hide. And there was the museum itself. He
could be in there.

Opting for the courtyard, I moved north, past the
round sculpture, looking right and left into the grassy
mound beside the divider. The whole courtyard was silent now, except for my footsteps slapping on the grass. I
glanced down into the depression by the west wall. It
was all in shadow, almost black. I couldn't even make
out the benches. I started down, stopped, waited. Nothing moved. I turned, ran back up the tiers to the north
wall, leapt to the top and looked down into the emptiness on the far side.

From my vantage point I glanced down the tiers,
turned to check the tinted glass of the museum. There
were still plenty of places to hide. I moved back toward
the entrance to cut off any escape, wishing I had my
flashlight.

From behind me came steps.

Whirling, I got set to run.

It was Howard, abreast the south exterior wall. I sighed. Another miss. The best we could say was that the rear-view mirror was still on the car.

Starting toward Howard, I heard a noise behind me.

Howard took off, past me around the divider and out of sight. I followed. My sandals slipped on the wet grass. I fell, scrambled up, ran to the dark alcove. Grunts, pants came from the bottom. No one was visible. Forms became clearer. I jumped down. Howard howled. The thief had him down. The thief was on top of him. His hands were on Howard's neck.

"Get off!" I leapt down, and stopped dead.

The thief was kissing Howard.

Chapter

"You're a woman!" I pulled the thief off Howard.

Howard scrambled up. When his face hit the light it was as red as his hair. He shook his head and kept shaking it as he stared at the young woman.

Now that the shock had passed I felt a grin taking hold. I turned away from the woman and whispered to Howard, "A new method of subduing a suspect? Is that in the Department manual?"

Ignoring that, Howard turned to the woman. She was young, probably not twenty, but there was an innocence to her expression that made her look younger still and very vulnerable, hardly the type one would expect for a thief.

"You've been stealing things from my car, haven't you?" Howard demanded.

The girl smiled shyly at him. "Yes."

"An aerial, a license plate, the tail-light reflectors, and whatever you were going after tonight. Right?"

She was still smiling. "Yes."

"You still got the stuff?"

"Oh, yes. I wouldn't give it away. It's all in my room. Do you want to see it?" It was a come-on, junior-high-school style.

"What's your name?" I asked.

She turned to me, surprised. She'd forgotten I was there. Her whole rapturous gaze had been aimed at Howard. But now that she looked directly at me, I realized I had seen her before. She'd been at Priester's—the Miss Muffet who'd been staring at Howard.

"Daisy Arbutus."

"What's your real name, Daisy?"

She looked adoringly back at Howard. "I don't have to tell you that, do I?"

"Yeah, you do." Howard was getting the picture. He turned redder still.

"I always go by Daisy. A friend of mine, a man, he called me Daisy Arbutus. I don't like my old name. It's not me."

I put a hand on her arm. "Show me some identification, Daisy. A driver's license."

"I don't drive."

"Library card."

"I don't read real good."

"MediCal card?" It was a stab.

But she smiled, pleased to be able to produce something, and began digging through her pockets until she pulled out a card with rows of MediCal stickers on it. "Harriet Turner," it said. Glancing back at her, I had to admit Daisy Arbutus fit her better.

"Where do you live, Daisy?"

"On Dana," she said, pointing west of Telegraph.

"Okay. You'll get to ride in Officer Howard's car, or what remains of it."

"With Seth?" she asked dreamily.

"With Seth Howard."

I glanced at Howard, waiting for him to do something, but he just looked awkward. He looked like an older brother at a thirteen-year-old's pajama party.

"Daisy," I said as we headed toward the car, "what

about the Ranier Hotel, the one you ran through the other afternoon?"

"I don't live there."

"Why did you go through it?"

"It was easy."

I waited.

"I used to get letters there."

"Why?"

"Well, people do."

"It's a mail drop, isn't it?" That didn't surprise me. Mail drop was doubtless one of its more legitimate functions. I remembered noticing the hotel didn't have individual mailboxes. It wasn't that type of place. If you wanted to get your mail there you made sure you were waiting when the postman came—a time-consuming ritual, but time was one thing the Ranier's tenants had in abundance. And with the manager who made himself scarce, it was the perfect set-up for a mail drop.

"I guess it's a drop. But I didn't do anything against the law. I mean I just got letters from my father there because it was easy. I was living around, you know. Like I couldn't tell him an address."

"Do a lot of people get mail there?"

"I think so. There's a big table in the lobby and the mailman leaves the letters there. People wait for the mailman."

Thinking of Anne's cases with that address, I asked, "What kind of mail did people get?"

Daisy shook her long curls. "I didn't look."

"Are you sure?"

She stared at me, her brown eyes wide, puppy-like. "Oh, yes. I know it's good to stay out of people's business."

We were at the car. Howard opened the back door and motioned Daisy in. Shutting it, he moved back a few steps.

No longer able to control my grin, I said. "A shrine to you in auto parts. I'll bet she has your picture from the paper on top."

"Shit. It'll be the next century before I hear the end of this."

I could envision the station, with the entire staff making cracks.

"Look on the bright side. You could be short and ugly, then no one would pay any attention at all."

"Wonderful. You know, Jill, Lieutenant Davis isn't going to be laughing. Particularly when this hits the papers, he won't be laughing."

It was true. Rarely had the lieutenant laughed about things connected with police work. And theft of any kind certainly would not move him to mirth.

"I'd give a lot to keep this quiet," Howard said.

We stood silently, as Daisy looked through the wire mesh in the squad car, eyeing the radio, the log book, the odometer.

Glancing from her to the street, Howard said, "I'll bet she has access to a lot of information."

"You're right, she probably does. I'd like to know more about that hotel, and about the welfare scene here, particularly as it relates to Anne Spaulding. Daisy could be a big help."

The frown lines around Howard's mouth disappeared. "She could return the aerial and stuff. She could say it was a prank—it was, sort of—and we could swap the information you get for dropping the theft charges. Okay?"

"Sounds good to me."

Looking back at Daisy, who was now gazing up at him, Howard said, "I guess I'm the one to ask her."

"I'm sure whatever information she has is yours." Still grinning, I started for my own car. With luck I could change back into uniform and still have time to find Ermentine Brown. She had lived in one of the Avenue hotels. If the hotels were drops, Ermentine would know what went through them.

It was nearly dark, but it was also Thursday. Any weekend is a big sales time on the Avenue and Thursday nights are the start. Street artists still manned tables, their wares illuminated by the yellow glare from the streetlights and the harsher fluorescent lights flowing from the stores.

I hurried along, glancing at each table, hoping Ermentine Brown would be there.

I was nearly to campus when I spotted her, sitting on a canvas chair behind her card table of feather necklaces. Her wide Afro wig sparkled in the light and her brown face had the illusion of softness.

Two young women glanced at the jewelry but Ermentine Brown didn't look up.

"Ms. Brown," I said.

"Huh?" It was a growl. And seeing me, her face tightened to match her voice.

"I'm Officer Smith, remember?"

"Yeah, I remember. Come by later. I gotta take care of business."

"This is business, too. You can get your neighbor to watch things for you."

"You tellin' me how to run my place?"

"Look, Ms. Brown, I have to talk to you—now. Make whatever arrangements you want. Or we can talk here."

"Here? Yeah, that's cool." She settled back in the chair.

"You said you'd lived in a hotel off Telegraph. When was that?"

"Why you want to know?"

"I'm still checking on Spaulding."

"Well, what the hell—"

"Just answer the question."

She shrugged. " 'Bout a year ago."

"With your kids?"

Her jaw jutted out. "Look, you checkin' for the welfare people? Are you trying to say I let my kids live in one of those places? Listen, woman, I wouldn't let my kids in there if it was snowing outside. Those hotels are full of winos and junkies and whores."

The fact that the clientele was not screened was hardly news to me. I'd had enough nuisance calls from the hotels to know what kind of people lived in them. I leaned gingerly on the edge of the card table. Ermentine Brown eyed my rump as it skirted her merchandise. Behind me, I could hear shoppers commenting on the necklaces, talking about coming back.

"You're ruining my business," Ermentine Brown complained. "I could have made ten dollars in this time. No one buys from a table with a cop on it."

"I'll be brief, if you'll answer my questions. When you lived there, was the hotel a drop?"

Her hand went to her lip and poised there, then fell to her lap. "Yeah. Sure."

"And now?"

"Right on. Everyone knows those places are drops. I'm surprised you don't—and you a *po*-lice officer."

"Do the eligibility workers at the welfare department know?"

"If they don't they should."

"And they send money there anyway?"

"Not without checking, they don't."

I raised an eyebrow.

"I mean, they come out, they look at your rent receipt, and they look at your room, with you in it."

"Anne Spaulding did that?"

"Believe it. She was the last one to trust you. I was hardly out of the welfare office and she was checkin' on me."

I made a note of the procedure. "It'd still be pretty easy to fake. All you'd need would be a friend living there, and a receipt book."

Ermentine Brown shrugged. "Maybe you're on the wrong side of the law."

As I headed back to the car, I wondered why Anne Spaulding had checked on Ermentine Brown and not on others. Was the rule intermittent? Or was she already aware that they didn't live there? I needed to know the policy. What was printed in the welfare manual I could read, but what I had to find out was how the workers translated that into practice. And for that I'd let Mona Liebowitz start helping me.

Chapter

17

In fifteen minutes I was knocking on the door of the house in front of which I had left Mona Liebowitz. But Mona didn't live in a house either. She lived in the "rear cottage." I was beginning to wonder if this type of living arrangement were a prerequisite of welfare work.

I hurried up the driveway, but the backyard held no cottage, no rear flat attached to the main house, only a garage that had been amateurishly converted to a dwelling. I knocked on one of the double doors.

"Mona," I called.

It was a moment before she pushed open the door and invited me in. One ceiling light shone dully on the grayed cement walls. The room held a threadbare over-stuffed chair, a queensize mattress covered with an old sampler quilt and shelves of record albums that extended over the entire wall. The stereo equipment looked expensive. Maybe Mona *had* been casing the Bank of America.

"That's some collection," I said.

Mona collapsed in the chair. "It keeps me broke, but it's worth it. Sit."

The floor was covered with worn oriental rugs and several large throw pillows, and despite its general shabbiness, the room seemed cozy. It suited Mona. Mona and this place: there was the internal consistency Skip Weston had mentioned. If Mona had made the smallest effort to fit in a Bank of America, if she'd worn a brassiere or even a jacket, Sri Fallon would never have noticed her. All she'd have needed to do was disguise her body; she had a face that simply was not memorable. With proper costuming she could have enjoyed internal consistency anywhere.

I looked at the shelf-after-shelf of albums. Could they have been bought with only an eligibility worker's salary? Or was Mona also taking bribes? Or blackmail? Mona had been arguing with Alec and Anne. She was making a considerable effort to find out about Anne. Could that have been why Mona was at the bank, because Anne was? Could Mona have been blackmailing Anne?

I sat on one of the pillows. "Mona, what do you know about the Telegraph Avenue transient hotels?"

She frowned. "They're a nuisance, for one thing. We get a lot of clients in those hotels. You have to go out and see them. Then two weeks later they move and you have to verify residence again."

"How do you normally do that?"

"Rent receipt."

"And in the hotels?"

"There we do both. We need the visit to see that the clients are actually there and we have to see the rent receipt to make sure they're not just using someone else's room."

"But how do you know the receipt isn't faked?"

Mona pulled a bare foot up under her, adjusting herself with the movements of a cat in the sun. "The landlords cooperate. We're their major source of revenue.

They'd better be straight with us. They use special receipt books. If you saw one you'd know what I mean."

"Do you take the receipt from the client? Could I find one in a case folder?"

"It's optional. I don't but some workers do. That means you'd have to plow through all the case folders till you lucked across one."

I could imagine Alec Effield's reaction to my doing that!

"Or you could check with someone who's lived there. Welfare clients keep everything." She paused, watching as I wrote down what she had said. "Jill, why are you asking all this?"

"I have to know the precedure to judge what people tell me." It was hardly a satisfactory answer. Mona had been helpful. I was sorry I couldn't level with her. "This is going to sound a little strange—"

"Good, I like strange things."

"Okay. Where do you bank?"

Mona sat up straight. "Jesus. That's not the type of strange I had in mind."

I waited but she didn't go on.

"Do you have an account at Bank of America?"

It was a moment before she said, "You're really serious, aren't you?"

"Yes."

"Well, I'm kind of embarrassed to admit it, but I don't have an account anywhere. I have albums." She glanced toward the rear wall.

"You've never considered an account?"

"You sound like my mother." She pushed herself up, walked over to the stereo and turned the record over. Leaving it poised silently on the turntable, she said, "Listen, what do you think of Anne and Donn Day?"

Recalling Fern Day's lack of an alibi, I decided to see where this diversion would lead. "Did Anne have something going with him?"

"I don't know. It's possible. At least Fern acted like she thought it was possible."

"How do you mean?"

"It's no big thing, but Fern used to listen to Anne's phone calls. That's not hard in our office."

"But Anne had that little room in the back."

"She didn't before Nat Smith came. She used to have his desk, right next to Fern. All Fern had to do was pay attention to every word Anne said." Mona had paused momentarily as she said Nat's name. I was again thankful that, whatever his reason, he'd never mentioned his ex-wife was a cop.

"Did Donn call Anne?" I asked.

"I don't know, but I wouldn't be surprised. Anne and Donn were really suited, birds of a feather, or whatever cliche suits you. Donn's after anything with tits. Seems to think it's his artistic right. I don't know if he follows through or just puts on the act." Her skeptical expression suggested a vote for the latter. "One time I was at his studio to meet Fern. She was due in twenty minutes and he came on to me! Maybe I should have taken him up on it just to see what he'd do."

Pereira, Mona, probably Anne Spaulding. Donn Day certainly had catholic taste.

Mona laughed.

"What?"

"It'd just be so fitting. Donn's after women for the body count. And Anne—mind you, this is just my observation —was a sophisticated tease. She might tantalize Donn Day, but I'll bet she wouldn't bother to sleep with him. She wouldn't have become another body on his list."

"Do you think that would be Fern's assessment?"

"It's what she fears, but she'd die before she'd admit it."

I stood up.

"Do you have to go?" Mona asked, pushing herself up and moving to the door. "Well, come back again."

"One more thing," I said as I got to the door. "You never did tell me what you were doing at the bank."

"Well, uh . . ." Mona looked wistfully at the albums.

"Yes?"

"Well, what it was was that I made a difficult decision. I suppose you could call it a rite of passage."

"In the bank?"

"The decision was here, the implementation was in the bank." Mona moved back to a large pillow and sank down. "I decided it was time I saved money. I mean, I am twenty-five years old. I probably have more albums than half of Berkeley. There are some I haven't played in months. I can't just go on buying every sound that appeals to me. I have to grow up, be responsible, like my mother said. So, I decided to open an account."

"You were in the bank on the first of the month. You don't get paid till the tenth."

"I know. It was a bad move. Not because of my paycheck—I was going for information that day. I mean, I didn't know what I'd need to open an account. I'd never had one, not even a savings account as a child. But I'd forgotten what a zoo the bank is on the first, with every welfare client in there cashing checks."

"And?" I leaned back against the doorway, looking down at Mona.

"And I gave up." She sat forward, as if the remembrance of defeat cheered her. "You can probably tell that I had real mixed emotions about the whole project. Giving it up wasn't hard."

"But you went back to the bank again on the first of the next month."

Mona laughed. "Yes. Same project. I forgot about the first of the month again. Or maybe I just wanted to sabotage the plan. Or maybe all the clients calling about money on the first had brought the issue to my mind. When I got there, the bank was jammed, but I did force myself to at least pick up brochures." She laughed again. "And I rewarded myself with three albums on the way home that night. You want to hear one?"

"And that was the only reason you were in the bank?"

Mona looked startled. "Yes. It was a big thing, for me."

I waited, but Mona did not go on. Then I said good night, and left.

I didn't believe Mona. I couldn't prove her story wasn't true; considering Mona, it could have been. Still, I doubted it.

The stereo started. The sounds of the Preservation Hall Jazz Band floated out over the driveway.

In the car, I opened the window and sat listening to the music, contemplating the case. I reviewed my notes. And I wondered: What had Anne Spaulding done with her clients' rent receipts? There was no indication in any of the case folders I had seen. I hadn't thought to ask Ermentine Brown if Anne had kept her receipt, and I certainly didn't want to tackle her again to find out.

Perhaps, I thought, I'd have more success with Yvonne McIvor.

As I drove south, I asked myself . . . was I wasting my time detailing Anne's abuses at the welfare department when her death might have been a simple crime of passion? Had Fern killed her to avoid losing Donn? Nothing in Anne's bloodstained living room suggested otherwise.

But McIvor would take only a few minutes. She was a loose end. And her apartment was on the way.

Unlike on my previous visit, there was no soul music blaring from Yvonne McIvor's apartment. I rang the bell.

"Who's there?"

"Officer Smith."

"What do you want?" the angry voice yelled through the closed door.

"I won't keep you long."

"Okay. Okay. Just a minute."

The minute stretched into three or more. I wondered what Yvonne had been doing at nine o'clock on a Thursday night that would take this long to recover from. Was she letting a john out the back door or trying to air out the smell of grass? I glanced down the dark stairway, again noting what an ominous, closed place it was. Yvonne McIvor was lucky no one had hidden here, waiting for her return some night.

When she opened the door, the music started, but it was turned low. She was still wearing the green dashiki she'd had on this morning. Her face was tense, her small features drawn down in a scowl.

"Are you alone?" I asked.

She planted her hands on her hips. "Yeah. Why you askin'? The welfare don't care 'bout men friends no more."

Walking in, I said, "You used to live at a hotel off Telegraph. I need to see your rent receipt."

"Why didn't you look before? You were here long enough. I don't keep shit forever."

"It was only from last month. You keep things the welfare might want longer than that."

"Yeah, most stuff. But I don't have that. I mailed it to Miz Spaulding. She said she had to send it to the copy machine at the main welfare office in Oakland. And when Miz Spaulding take, honey, she don't always give back, you understand?"

"Didn't she send you anything? A receipt for it? A note?"

"Maybe. Like I said, that was more than a month ago. I moved again. When I moved outa there I threw out all the stuff from that dive."

"Okay," I said, "then let me see what you got from Anne Spaulding in return for the rent receipt on this apartment."

"Why?"

"You told me you mailed her your rent receipt on Saturday. It's Thursday now. She must have sent something back to you."

When Yvonne McIvor didn't answer, I said, "I'd hate to have to start over on this."

She stood, shoulders moving to the hard beat of the music, eyes averted as if considering whether the effort of searching was worth the prospect of being rid of me. "Okay. Okay. I'll look. I got so much shit spread here, I don't know where nothin' is. You better take a seat."

I sat, watching her look in drawers, among piles of

papers. As she headed toward the kitchen I followed and leaned against the doorway while she went through the cabinets.

"Don't seem like it would be here, but I can't say no." She headed back toward the living room, stopped. "I gotta go. Bladder infection." With that, she rushed to the bathroom, grabbing her purse.

I glanced into the bedroom, catching the reflection of the room in the marbleized mirror squares that covered the far wall. Sheets and blankets hung from the bed, clothes lay in piles on the floor, intermingled with copies of *Ebony, Jet,* and a skiwear catalog. On the dresser were several pairs of long beaded earrings, a parched ivy plant, and a pile of batik scarves that drooped over a cheap picture frame containing a newspaper photo of a young black girl—Yvonne's niece or sister? As I moved closer to check the resemblance, the toilet flushed.

Had I made a mistake in letting her in the bathroom alone? Had she flushed something I'd needed?

I had just gotten back to my chair when Yvonne Mc-Ivor hurried in.

"When you got this bladder stuff, you gotta go fast." Perching next to me, she held out a paper. "I didn't waste no time. I emptied my purse out. That's what I shoulda done first. I keep all my business there. Everyone on the welfare does." She patted the bulging plastic purse. "And, honey, you are in luck."

I took the paper. On it was a statement, on NCR paper with the county logo, acknowledging that a rent receipt for the date in question had been submitted to the welfare department. The signature said, "Anne Spaulding."

It looked legitimate, but I'd have to check it. And the one who could tell me was Fern Day.

Chapter

18

"That's Anne's signature," Fern Day said, settling in the one comfortable chair. By her arm was a jar of peanuts, half gone, and a glass of what appeared to be sherry. Her living room walls were covered with canvasses—Donn Day's. In the dining room stood an easel, surrounded by rags, tubes of paint, a bottle of linseed oil, and brushes soaking in a can. The smells of paint and turpentine filled both rooms.

I sat opposite her on a church pew. It was after ten o'clock. That late night last night was catching up with me. My eyes wanted to close and even the hard surface of the pew was inviting. Inhaling deeply, I said, "I'm going to ask you again, where were you the night Anne Spaulding . . . Monday night?"

Fern's dark penciled eyebrows rose. Her hand moved toward the peanuts, but she caught it and brought it back to the chair, empty.

When she didn't speak, I said, "I know you were at Alec Effield's party. But after that . . ."

She bit her cheek, kneading the flesh between her

teeth. I could almost see the conflict as she decided between the truth and a stubborn reiteration of what she had told me.

"I was home with Donn."

"That's not what he says."

"Donn must be mistaken."

"He's not. He was at the gallery preparing for the show. The workmen were with him all evening."

"They must have meant another night."

"No, they didn't. Come on, Fern, why did you say you were with Donn?"

She opened her mouth to protest, but she must have seen the futility of it, for she let it shut, and sat staring over my head. She ran her teeth over her lower lip, biting hard enough to leave the skin red.

"Fern?"

She said nothing.

"Were you protecting Donn? Did you think he might have been with Anne?"

"No. No. Donn is just friends with Anne."

"That's not what I've heard."

Her head started to shake; the loose chin quivered.

"Look, Fern, you know Donn comes on to women, don't you? Where it counts, you know. Don't waste energy pretending."

Her hand went for the peanuts. She looked at it as it poised over the container. Then she picked up the jar and flung it to the floor. "How can he?" she screamed. "I've given him everything. I take care of him; I love him; he's my life! How can he do this?"

Her face was deep red. Tears hung precariously at the corners of her eyes. In her hands she knotted the crimson cloth of her caftan.

On the floor between us the peanut jar, unbroken, rocked back and forth, mocking Fern.

I asked, "Do you think he was sleeping with Anne?"

"I don't know. Anne, the girl at the gallery, the girl at the paint store, any flighty little blonde with . . . with . . ."

"With what?"

"With a skinny little body, like yours!"

The tears rolled freely. She raised an arm to wipe them, stared at the hanging fat, and dropped the arm to her side.

"Fern," I said softly, "it's better to face the truth, even when it seems unbearable." It had taken a divorce to teach me that. "Crying it out would be best, but I have to find a murderer. I don't have time to let you cry. Pull yourself together."

Fern looked up, shocked. Among counselors, and Fern Day had made it clear she so considered herself, cutting off tears was unheard of.

Allowing an edge to my voice, I said, "You can't think of yourself now." When she didn't respond, I softened my voice. "I need your help."

The tears continued to roll, but she steadied her body and looked through them at me.

"Why did you think that Donn might be at Anne's that night?"

Fern stared unmoving, then the words poured out. "Anne left the party early. She said she had to stop at the store. I couldn't be sure it wasn't a ruse. I had to know. Don't you see, I couldn't have Donn sleeping with a woman who worked with me. I couldn't have her leering at me, mocking me, thinking of me as a patsy, fat, middle-aged patsy who provides the bread for her lover."

I said gently, "What did you do?"

"I went there. I went to Anne Spaulding's."

"When?"

"Right after I left Alec's."

"Did you go into Anne's apartment?"

"Oh, no. I wouldn't do that. I didn't . . . didn't want to burst in."

"What did you do?"

"I parked across the street. There was a big tree. It cut out the light. My car was dark. I sat and watched."

"And? Try to put yourself back there."

Fern nodded obediently. I realized this was a technique with which a counselor probably was familiar.

"I sat there in the silence. No, wait, it wasn't silent. There was this terrible racket coming from the apartment above Anne's. I thought maybe the tenant was remodeling."

I suppressed a smile.

"Then Anne's door opened. Nat Smith came out. He wasn't in a hurry. He just strolled down the steps, got into his car."

My breath caught. He had been there. He had dropped the pewter pen. And what else had he done?

"And?" I prompted. The word sounded like a croak, but Fern didn't seem to notice.

"I watched Nat. He sat in the car for a few minutes. His car was in front of mine, farther from the apartment building. He sat there. I watched him. I wondered what had gone on in there. And then his car pulled away."

Forcing myself to concentrate on Fern's actions, to ask questions in sequence instead of speculating about Nat, I said, "And then what next?"

"When I looked back I could see the outlines of two figures in Anne's window."

"Two figures? You saw Nat leave. Did you see someone go in?"

"No."

"So the other person was inside all the time, then?"

"Yes. No. Wait. I don't know. I watched Nat Smith as he left Anne's. I watched him sit in the car. I watched just him. It was a few minutes, like I said. Someone could have come to Anne's door and I wouldn't have seen him. I don't know."

"Okay. The two outlines in Anne's window, describe them. Take your time."

"One was Anne. I could tell by the way she moved. The other . . . the other was a man. He wasn't much bigger than Anne. He had long hair, long gray hair. His suit was brown, old. It didn't fit."

"You saw that through the curtain?"

"Oh, no. I just saw shadows then. But the man came out. I saw him as he came out."

"Tell me about it."

"He was very angry. He slammed the door. His hands were in fists. Then he went upstairs. That was before the black woman came down the driveway."

"Wait. Slow down. The man came out of Anne's and . . ."

"He started down the steps. Then he spun around and went back to Anne's door. But he didn't knock. He just stood looking at it. Then he went upstairs."

I wrote quickly to get it all down. "Have you seen him before or since?"

Fern's eyes tightened, as if trying to hold the picture of the man. "I don't know. I can't be sure. He seems familiar, but a lot of people look alike in Berkeley."

It was true, but it wouldn't matter. Despite Fern's observation, there couldn't be too many gray-haired men with baggy brown suits who were followers of Sri Fallon. "What about the black woman? Did she come out of the upstairs apartment?"

"No. She came down the driveway."

"Down the driveway from where? From Anne's back door? From the path that leads to the next street?"

"I don't know. She was just in the driveway when I saw her."

"What did she look like?"

"She had a big Afro. She was in the shadows. All I could really see was her hair."

"Did the man see her?"

"Oh, no. He'd gone upstairs."

"Do you think they were together?"

Her head shook slowly. Her eyes remained glazed. "I didn't see her inside."

"Could she have been in there without you seeing her?"

"I guess. But just Anne and the man were arguing. They must have been ignoring the black woman if she was there."

What about Nat when he had been in the apartment—

had he ignored them both? Or had Anne seen Nat, the old man, and then the black woman sequentially, like customers at the butcher's? I asked, "What did the black woman do when she left?"

"She walked down College, south toward the intersection, at Ashby."

"Fern, how much time elasped after the man came out of the front door and the woman left?"

Her eyes focused; she looked down, directing her attention somewhere left of my knees. "Maybe five minutes. No longer."

"And then what happened, after the woman left?"

"I watched the window for a moment or two. Nothing was going on. Then I realized how late it was—it was ten o'clock. I had told Donn I'd be home by nine. I didn't want to explain where I was, so I hurried home. I hoped he wouldn't notice." She paused. "He didn't."

"Is there anything else you remember?"

Her body sagged. It looked like a pile of crimson rags. "No, that's all."

"And then you came straight home?"

"Yes."

"Did you see anyone?"

"No. I didn't see anyone. I came home and went to bed."

Looking at her, I wondered if she could have made it all up. The scene she described didn't make any sense—Nat, the gray-haired man, and the black woman, hanging around Anne's apartment.

It was easier to believe that Fern had driven to Anne's, walked in and beaten her with the lamp—a crime of passion, with the clothes torn and discarded deliberately to make it look like a sex killing.

I sighed. It was going to take some legwork—and some luck—to find out.

Using the kitchen phone, I called Sri Fallon and told him I knew the devotee he had mentioned. He was the gray-haired, brown-suited man Fallon had been attempting to calm in the welfare office, Ermentine Brown's "old dude" who'd threatened to go right to Anne's apartment, the alcoholic who blamed Anne for his friend Tad's over-dose.

"He's Quentin Delehanty, isn't he?" I asked.

Fallon wasted no time trying to deny it. He merely reminded me of my promise to treat Delehanty fairly.

Chapter

During the day Telegraph Avenue is jammed with people: street artists like Ermentine Brown sitting behind their displays of feather necklaces, tie-dyed T-shirts, stained-glass panels; students and former students wandering along fingering the merchandise; street people hanging out in coffee houses or squatting along the walls watching time pass. The sidewalks are overflowing then. Now at nearly midnight the Avenue had an eerie yellow glow from the streetlights bouncing off the bare macadam, and small groups of regulars made their way slowly down the empty sidewalks.

I parked the car in a red zone outside Quentin Delehanty's hotel and made my way past the empty lobby. Even now music came from all directions. The songs smashed into one another, grating as they separated, only to come back at each other. It was lucky for Delehanty that he drank.

I knocked on his door. There was no answer. I knocked, pounded and then tried the door only to find it locked. The man in the next room stuck his head out and, seeing me, withdrew it quickly. I followed him and, with a minimum of pressure, found out that he'd seen Delehanty go out at nine.

Leaving the hotel, I walked the half block to the Avenue. In the daytime the street is congested with cars slowing to turn, with drivers stopping abruptly to chat with pedestrian friends. No one uses Telegraph for a thoroughfare. Even now, when a driver could cruise the street unhindered, no one thought of it. And with the yellow glow of the streetlights and the abandoned street, the empty Avenue looked like a sepia-toned photograph.

I walked quickly toward campus, checking in the few coffee houses that were still open, looking in doorways, peering down alleyways. Finding nothing, I hurriedly surveyed the far side of the street, walking at almost a jog. But it was clear that Quentin Delehanty was nowhere on the Avenue. He was probably at some friend's place, drinking. He could be wandering home soon. He could be there for the night. After all, he had few demands on his time.

Digusted at the waste of an hour, I climbed back into the car and cruised slowly up the Avenue, mostly for form's sake; I didn't really expect to see Delehanty.

I'd imagined by now Delehanty would have told me what had occurred in Anne's apartment Monday night. He was there; Anne was there; the black woman was there; and Nat.

Nat! I stepped sharply on the gas and headed for Nat's house across town in north Berkeley. Normally it would be a twenty-minute drive; this late, I'd make it in little more than ten.

Nat hated to be woken up. Too bad. If he'd been honest in the beginning he could have slept undisturbed. If he had a decent conscience, *it* would be keeping him awake.

I pulled the wheel sharply as I rounded the corner to the house. The tires squealed. Was I taking on the role of conscience for the entire block?

A bit sheepishly I got out of the car. It was a pleasant street of stucco houses, inhabited by small families. Most windows were dark now. But at Nat's the light was on. I knocked and in a minute the door opened. Nat's hair hung disheveled as it had in the library, and behind him, beyond the darkened living room, I could see his dissertation, notes, and reference books spread all across the dining room table. The house looked the same—a small four-room square, living room and dining room on the south side, bedroom and kitchen on the north. I hadn't been here in six months, but as I stepped inside, those months disappeared, and with them all the objectivity I'd worked to attain.

"You lied to me. You were in Anne's apartment Monday night. What happened there?"

"What?"

"Fern Day saw you leave."

"So she was the one in the car. She must have been spying on Anne. Jesus Christ!"

From the kitchen came the smell of frying eggs. Omelets in the middle of all-nighters had been one of Nat's specialties. He must have noted the smell now, for he started toward the kitchen.

Was Nat's defensive reaction a clumsy attempt to cover guilt? Or was this just Nat's reaction to me?

Following, I said, "What happened in Anne's apartment Monday night? What did the old man do? And the black woman?"

Nat looked at me, incredulous. "There was no man or woman there. Just Anne and me."

"Fern saw the man."

"I don't care what Fern Day may think she saw, or may have seen later. God knows how long Fern Day would sit outside Anne's, spying. Boy, that's just like her—voyeurism. But when I was inside, there was no one but Anne and me. And, Jill, I was only there ten minutes, fifteen at the outside. We talked. I left. Anne was fine."

"I'm assuming you're telling the truth now. This will all be cross-checked."

He spun around. "Is that why you had that oaf out badgering Owen? You're prying into my life, aren't you?"

I had forgotten Nat's detestation of Howard. They'd met only twice, and then briefly, but when things deteriorated between us, Howard had come to symbolize the police department in Nat's mind and all the hostility he hadn't focused on me he'd aimed at Howard.

"You left me no choice. You lied."

Nat moved closer and glared down. "I won't have my friends hounded by the police. And I won't have you checking up on me."

"You asked me to investigate this as a favor, and then you lied. Nat, you are a suspect."

"No, Jill, Anne was fine when I left her. You're just angry because I didn't tell you every move I made."

I knew that tone and the multitude of references inherent in that statement. I was too familiar with this tack —the problem, according to Nat, was not his dishonesty; the problem was my anger. I pushed the memories from my mind. "Why didn't you tell me you were there?"

He stepped back, sighed professorially. "Because, Jill, I knew you would create a scene, like you're doing now."

I took a breath. Another familiar tack. "Nat, you can't lie to the police."

"I will not have you checking up on me!"

Gearing my voice to the impersonal tone that always infuriated him, I said, "Then you will have to move out of Berkeley. The Department isn't going to change its procedure to suit your delicate nature."

"Jill, I will not have—"

"File a complaint."

The blood vessels throbbed against Nat's temples. His teeth pressed hard together. "I can't trust you. I asked you to see what happened to Anne as a friend and—"

"File another complaint!"

"This isn't business. This is personal . . ."

"It's not personal. Nothing's personal now. You were—"

He spun and slammed out the front door. In a moment I heard the car door bang closed.

I turned back toward the pan in which his omelet was

burning. The center was black and around it ran the goo from whatever he had in the center. I stared down, seething, as I had so many times. His demeaning accusations! The gall that he would think I cared who he spent his time with! And all this, and he hadn't even seen Delehanty, much less the black woman.

The engine of Nat's car ground and started; the tires squealed as he pulled away.

Obviously he was even more furious than I. In his rage, Nat had erased the last year. He had forgotten I no longer lived here.

I glared at the open door. I could have run into the street and screamed after him, loud enough to wake any neighbor who wasn't already up and angry.

Instead, I scraped the runny blackened eggs onto a plate, carried them into the dining room, and emptied them onto Nat's dissertation notes.

Chapter

20

It was after noon when I woke up Friday. Outside the sun shone; the backyard lawn had been mown but I hadn't heard the noise. Even after nine hours of sleep I was still tired.

I dragged myself out of the sleeping bag, pulled the bottom end up over my pillow and shuffled to the closet. Pairs of jeans, pale and navy, new, frayed, heavily patched, hung from two hooks. T-shirts and sweaters were suspended from another. Only a cashmere sweater, my one skirt, and my special-occasion dress merited the three hangers. When I'd first moved in seven months ago, there was some excuse, but by now the general slovenliness of the place was an embarrassment. Maybe when my day off came I'd buy hangers, a tatami (I'd long since given up so formal a thought as a bed), sheets, towels, curtains, a decent rug . . .

I rooted through the clean T-shirts that had fallen onto the heap on the closet floor, chose one that was nearly unwrinkled, grabbed jeans, and headed to the shower.

But I could put off thinking about the case only so

long. The suspects, the possibilities, the things I hadn't
done, those I shouldn't have, washed over me with the
hot water. I didn't want to consider it all alone. Using my
one Holiday Inn towel, I dried off. Then, plugging in the
phone, I called Howard. He'd had breakfast (five hours
earlier) but said he'd meet me for lunch.

At one-thirty when the lunch crowd had left most
places, Priester's was still full. Students were drinking
coffee before two o'clock classes, or dawdling over
lunch, pushing their food around their plates while leaning forward in discussion of the University's involvement in nuclear weaponry, of black holes, of Zen and
Molière. A pair of women, with bags of purchases filling
the seats next to them, was in our regular place.

"At least we're not in uniform," Howard said, sitting
down by the front window.

But familiarity had its perks. Two cups of coffee appeared and our order—pancakes for me and cheeseburger, fries, salad, and strawberry pie for Howard—
was taken immediately.

"No donut?" Howard asked. "You sure wholesome
food won't ruin your digestion? Not that pancakes are so
healthy. You could at least have an egg."

"Actually, I couldn't," I said. "I really could not face an
egg this morning." I told Howard about interviewing Nat
and the eggs and the dissertation notes.

Howard's face reddened. He howled. People at nearby
tables stared. I realized I, too, was laughing.

"Nobody," Howard said finally, "could appreciate that
more than me. If I could have suspended him by the
heels and shaken the truth out of him I would have. That
interview with him this morning . . . well, let's just say
I can see why you divorced him."

"What did he tell you?"

"In words, nothing. In wariness, hesitations, looking
around, changing the subject, objecting—he said plenty."

"Did he tell you he was at Spaulding's apartment Monday night?"

"No, but I'm hardly surprised."

I related Fern Day's information and Nat's reaction. "I'm not looking forward to explaining this to the lieutenant."

Howard nodded. The food arrived.

Howard took a bite of his cheeseburger. "It won't do anything for your record, you know."

"I know."

"This case could be a great opportunity for you. There are still likely to be openings in Homicide. They'll take beat officers who have special assignment experience, ones who've shown they can handle themselves on the street, ones who can keep on top of interviews, who can deal with murders. With that case you had last month, if you finished off this one you'd be in good shape, very good shape."

Howard, who had been a motivating force in a sizeable drug bust in July and a fencing operation in September, was a likely candidate for upward movement himself. As ambitious as he was, his eagerness to consider my chances was a rare quality. "However," I said, "if I don't do anything with this case, if I have to explain that I took the initial report from my ex-husband and then didn't realize he was lying to me, it's not going to look good at all. And there's no way it should."

Howard forked his french fries. "I know. Listen, I don't have to write up my report on Nat till end of shift. Maybe you'll find the answer by then."

"No. There's no need to drag you into the messy end of this."

He swallowed the fries. "A couple hours, anything could cause that delay."

"No. The lieutenant knows we're friends. If this case is still in a shambles when it goes to Homicide, there'll be plenty of questions. You've got your career to think of."

"Jill, it doesn't matter what you say, unless you're planning to write my report for me. It'll be done when I get to it. It's not a priority."

"Howard—"

"Hi. Remember me? Daisy Arbutus?" The question was directed at Howard. He looked up and it took even him a moment to place this version of Daisy. She looked entirely different, like a little girl playing a vamp in a school play. She wore a clingy low-cut dress that exposed the ribs in her little-girl chest. Her eyes were outlined in stripes of black, white, and blue, and her curly hair was piled on her head.

"I went down to the police station, but they said you weren't on duty yet. I waited, then they told me you wouldn't come till three."

Howard glanced at me, a tacit reminder that we both had things we didn't want on our records. All he'd need would be Daisy taking up adoring residence in the waiting room.

I asked, "Did you have something to tell Officer Howard?"

Daisy turned, surprised. Already she'd forgotten I was there. "I'll tell *him.*" She slid into the seat next to him.

"Well, Daisy," Howard said, trying to avoid the adoring gaze, "what is it, then?"

"You said for me to watch the hotel and the people. I'm doing that."

Howard waited.

Daisy smiled proudly.

"Is that it?" he asked.

"I'm doing what you wanted." Her smile faded. "It is what you wanted?"

Howard nodded, playing for time. But there was no reason he should know what to ask her. It wasn't his case.

Daisy had been hanging around the hotel; she had to know *something.*

"What about the letters, Daisy," I asked. "Who picks the letters up there?"

Again she looked at me with surprise. "People. They come in. They get them off the table."

"What about special mail? Isn't it held somewhere?"

"I don't think so. No one said so." She looked at How-ard, worried, as if she should have the answer.

"Okay, Daisy," he said. "What about the mail on the first of the month, when checks arrive? Who comes then, did you ask?"

"I didn't ask, but Ronnie—he's a doper who lives right by the lobby—he told me all about it."

I took out my pad.

Turning full face to Howard, she said, "Ronnie says the lobby's really busy on the first. That's the day the welfare checks come. The people don't want to miss the mailman. They don't want to leave their money lying around. And—" She started to giggle.

"What?" he prompted.

"Well, Ronnie said it's real funny. No one wants to have anyone else see him, so all these people just hang around, and don't look at each other. No one talks. They just walk around in that little lobby, or in the hall. Ron-nie said—" She giggled again. "He said one day he went into the lobby and said, 'Hi, folks, why don't we all sit down and talk.' But they didn't think it was funny. I think it's funny, don't you?"

"Sure, Daisy," Howard said. "Now, these people, what did Ronnie say about them?"

"He's spent a lot of time watching them. There are four who come all the time. There's one Japanese guy. Ronnie says he has a moustache and looks very unscrewed, or something."

"Inscrutable?"

"Yeah. That's it. How do you say that?"

"In–scru–ta–ble," he said. "And who else?"

"Then there was an old guy who looks, well Ronnie says he looks like, wait, he looks like a poor man's Quen-tin Delehanty."

That, I thought, should be quite a sight.

"And there's a guy who's really hooked on something. Ronnie says he shakes bad, Officer Howard."

"And?"

"And then there's this woman."

"What kind of woman?"

"She's black. Ronnie says she's got a big Afro."

The black woman at Anne's apartment? Ermentine Brown? Yvonne McIvor? They both wore Afros. Did it all fit together? Controlling my excitement, I asked, "What did Ronnie say about her?"

Daisy turned abruptly toward me, her face pulled into a pout. "He said she seemed okay. He didn't say much about her."

"Anything else? Anything?"

Daisy seemed to be reaching down into unused pockets of memory. But she remained empty-handed. Distressed, she looked at Howard. When he smiled, she said, "Can I have some of your pie?"

"Sure, Daisy." He stood up. "You can finish the coffee too. I have to get ready for work. But you stay and eat."

I followed him as he hastened to the register, handed over a ten and headed for the door.

Outside, he said, "Maybe it was better to be losing aerials."

"No. Amazingly enough, Daisy's given me a lead."

"What?"

We were next to my car. "I have to think it through. I'll see you later."

"At dinner, then. My house."

"Okay." I got into the car, took out my pad, and began writing, trying to fit what Daisy had told me with what I already knew. Anne had been sending the checks to the hotel. The recipients of those checks didn't live there. Could the clients have moved and not notified Anne? No, not with the memos listing their new addresses stashed away ready to be put into the case folders. Had Anne continued sending checks to the hotels even when she knew the new addresses? But what did she get out of it— more kickbacks? Twenty dollars a month was hardly reason for murder.

Maybe when Pereira finished checking out these clients and their new addresses we'd find that those addresses were false. Maybe the clients were living in San

Francisco or Contra Costa County and collecting welfare checks there too? And the black woman, was it her job to pick up and deliver the checks and give Anne her cut?

I sat, tapping my pen. I felt sure the new address memos had been placed in the case folders after Anne was gone. Someone else—not Anne—had done that. Someone else knew about them. That someone had to be in on it. Who? Alec? Mona? Fern? Or Nat, Nat whom Anne had trained?

Or was I, I wondered as I put the pad back, getting caught up in those cases again and missing the obvious? Fern Day couldn't be sure the black woman had come from Anne's apartment. The last person she had actually seen in there was Quentin Delehanty.

Chapter

I ran up the hotel steps, through the lobby, to Delehanty's door and knocked.

There was no answer. He could be out still, crashing at some friend's place for a few drunken days. I banged on the door.

On the third round, I could hear footsteps and a hoarse, sleepy voice growling for a minute more.

"Come on, Delehanty!" I yelled. "I don't have all day."

"Yeah, yeah. I'm coming."

When the door opened I brushed past him before he had time to reconsider.

"I've got to talk to you, Delehanty," I said, leaning against the chipped dresser. It and the bed were the only items of furniture in the room. The walls had once been beige, but the paint was chipped now and swatches of blue, aqua, and rose showed through.

Delehanty slumped onto the bed, reaching under it for a nearly empty bottle. The movement to his mouth was surprisingly quick.

"It's about Anne Spaulding."

He drank again.

"Put that down. You're drunk enough as it is."

"Yeah," he said, taking another swallow.

I grabbed the bottle, spilling the deep red wine across the floor.

"Hey, lady, what . . ." He looked as if he wanted to say more but couldn't form the words.

"Tell me about Anne Spaulding."

He aimed his watery eyes up at me, his scowl melting into a glazed expression of amazement. His long gray hair was matted; his undershirt was grimy and days of sweat emanated from it.

"Anne Spaulding?"

He nodded, and kept nodding, rocking himself back close to sleep.

"Okay, Delehanty, get dressed."

His eyes opened. He said, "Huh," but it didn't come out like a question.

Taking out the card, I read him his rights, then I handed him his suit jacket, shoved one arm into it and pulled it around behind him, aiming the other arm toward the sleeve. Delehanty made no attempt either to help or hinder. He looked vaguely at the arm as if watching a movie on dexterity.

"Ouch," he exclaimed as I pushed it in.

"You may be gone overnight. Anything you want to take? Toothbrush?"

"Nah."

"Okay."

I headed for the door, still holding his arm.

As he stepped into the hall, he yelled, "Hey, take your hands off me! Lemme go!"

I tightened my grasp on his arm and looked nervously behind me. But no one came running. In this kind of hotel drunken cries were no special event. Still, handcuffs wouldn't hurt.

As I fastened them on his wrists, he yelled, "Lemme go! You're harassing me!"

"Calm down, Delehanty."

But if he heard me at all, it didn't faze him. He pushed through the outside door, dragging me along. "Lemme go! Help! Help!"

I hurried him down the stairs. A crowd was gathering at the street. I wished I'd called for back-up. It was too late now.

"Hey, cop, you're hurting him."

"He's just an old man," a bystander shouted.

"You didn't have to chain him."

The crowd grew. Delehanty, in an exhibit of unexpected strength, had dug in his heels, so that I was pulling him like I would a footlocker. His head hung, and he no longer bothered to protest.

Three burly men stood between the patrol car and me.

"Get out of my way," I demanded.

"Let him go," one said.

I stepped forward.

The trio moved in around me. "He's got rights, lady. Like you can't just drag him away, see."

"He can get a lawyer."

"Sure," the largest man said sarcastically.

The crowd moved closer.

I caught the man's eye. "Get out of the way."

His eyes wavered.

"Get out of the way," I repeated. "You're interfering with a police officer."

His heavy hands tensed at his sides. The crowd was hushed now, listening.

I said, "Do you want me to run your name through records? Do you want me to send to Sacramento and see what you've got outstanding?"

He stepped toward me.

Yanking Delehanty's arm, I jerked him forward as the man moved in, and when the man continued his step, it was into Delehanty.

Delehanty came alive, feet planted, body twisting and weaving. He bent forward and lurched, shoulder first, into the man's stomach. The man groaned.

The crowd burst into laughter.

Pulling open the back door of the patrol car, I shoved Delehanty in before another change of mood should arise. But as I glanced back at the crowd, there was no sign of hostile memory.

That was one advantage of being a woman officer—the macho hostility was diffused more easily.

Chapter

22

By the time I finished booking Delehanty it was past three-thirty.

He had passed out in the cell. I opened the door to the conference room slowly, expecting to make a stealthy entrance into staff meeting. But the room was empty. One less thing to explain.

I hurried to my desk. Pereira was sitting in my chair, finger tapping on the desk.

"You could almost be Lieutenant Davis, with that finger and that expression," I told her.

"I've been waiting since three. There was no staff meeting—the lieutenant had another session with the higher-ups. So I came here to tell you the news. I hate to wait when I have news."

I sat on the desk. "So?"

"Well," Pereira leaned back in the chair, taking her time. "I checked through all of Anne Spaulding's clients, checked every supposed new address. And do you know, Jill, not one of those women ever lived at those addresses? They don't get their mail there. No one's ever heard of them."

"Hmm. Interesting. Funny that Yvonne McIvor checked out okay, then. Run them through Files, will you?"

"Already done. Files comes up blank too. So do Files in the surrounding counties." Now she leaned forward. "So, Jill, they don't live at the hotels where they were getting money. They don't live at their new addresses where their money will be going. We have no record of them. They're not living in San Francisco or some other county around here. What does that make you think?"

"It sounds like these ladies don't exist."

Pereira gave a nod of agreement.

"Seems like the only real thing about them is their welfare checks. Twelve checks of two hundred dollars a month makes—"

"Twenty-four hundred dollars for the adults. Those five families could well add another twenty-five hundred. So, say five thousand a month. In a year that's sixty thousand, tax free."

"Enough to kill over," I said. "Even half that would be enough."

I hurried past the weary woman who sat uneasily on the metal chair of the waiting room and made my way by her children on the floor. In the former dining room, Fern was writing in a manila folder. Mona, at four-thirty, was getting ready to leave. Nat was across the room, but I didn't look his way and he didn't speak.

With a passing nod to Mona, I moved in on the kitchen-turned-office of Alec Effield.

Effield wore a red shirt with his beige pants; it made him look sallow.

"Mr. Effield, I want to talk to you about those cases of Anne's."

"No. I mean, I don't feel I should discuss them any further. I've been slipshod about confidentiality as it is."

"Mr. Effield, those women, the ones who supposedly

lived in the hotel, then moved to the new addresses in
the case folders—no one's ever heard of them. There's no
record of their existing at all."

"What?" He looked away.

I followed his eyes to the Suzanne Valadon sketch on
the wall. Beneath it the copy lay, still only half-com-
pleted. I doubted Effield had contributed a line today.

"How do you explain those non-existent people, Mr.
Effield?"

"Officer, you saw one of those clients, Yvonne McIvor."

"She exists, all right, but none of the others do."

Effield glanced nervously back at the Valadon sketch.
"There must be some mistake. You chose Yvonne McIvor
as the client you wanted to see, Officer. Maybe your department made some mistake with the other clients. Welfare clients and their neighbors don't always like to talk
to the police." But his wavering voice belied the excuse.
Effield looked so shaken I couldn't even be angry at his
attempt to shift the blame to us.

"Those clients don't exist. How can you explain that?"

He sank down in his chair. "I don't know. Let me
think. It just doesn't seem possible."

"Anne Spaulding was sending out money to people
who aren't there. There's only one place that money
could have been going, right?"

His head shook in a slow metronomic movement. "It
does look like it. But surely that couldn't be."

My glance landed on my watch: 4:22. I didn't have
time for Effield's bewilderment, not if I planned to find
Anne's murderer by eleven. "What's the procedure when
someone applies for welfare?"

Sluggishly, he focused on me. I could feel my fingers
tightening on the pen. "Well," he said, "the client comes
into the office, makes an appointment, and sees an eligibility worker."

"Does anyone keep a record of who applies?"

"The clerk."

"What happens to the record?"

"At the end of the month, the statistics are taken from

it and sent to Oakland and the original is either filed or thrown out."

"And yours were?"

Effield shook his head harder. "Thrown out."

I made a note. "So there's no way of knowing who came in to apply?"

"No."

"After they filled out the applications, then what?"

"There's a certain amount of verification necessary." Effield paused, then in a sudden motion opened the Yvonne McIvor file. "Since you've seen this already, I won't be breaking confidentiality." He pointed to a white, legal-size sheet on the left side of the folder. "Here you see that Anne has noted the birth-certificate number. If the client hadn't had a birth certificate, Anne would have requested a baptismal certificate and then sent to" —he glanced across the folder to another form listing the client's birthplace—"Springfield, for a copy."

"Here"—he pointed back to the first sheet—"is where we list any real property, personal property—"

"I think I understand. Mr. Effield, I'd like to see one of Anne's other cases—Janis Ulrick, or Linda Faye Miller."

"Why?"

"Because those clients don't exist. I want to see the differences between their folders and the McIvor folder."

"I really can't do that. I've stretched the rules as it is."

I sighed. I didn't have time to argue. "All right. Let it go. Now, if the worker says she's seen all the verification, then what?"

"She sets up the grant and sends it through."

"So you have only the worker's word that a client exists, right?"

"I suppose so. Unless someone's seen the client . . ." Effield's face had become paler yet. His head slumped into his hands. He sat motionless, sweat darkening the armpits of his red shirt. "Oh, God, maybe Anne did make dummy cases. How can I go on defending her? She could have. And I recommended her!"

I waited for him to continue.

"She used me as a reference. I knew her before. What will they think?"

"What about the dummy cases?"

"It could have been. If Anne set up dummies there's no way I would have known. She could have passed them off as real. They all could. Every worker in my unit could be making dummies."

"Do you think that's why she was killed?"

Effield's eyes widened. "Why? I mean, the dummies didn't do it. Anyone in administration, like myself, would be upset, but you don't kill because of fraud."

"Who could have known?" I asked.

"How can I say? I didn't know about the cases. How would I know who did?"

"Who was in a position to, from a logistical standpoint?"

Effield's fingers rubbed together. "I guess anyone in the office could have come across something."

"Like Mona?"

"Oh, no. Mona would have told me."

"Fern?"

"Oh, no. No."

"Nat Smith."

"Oh, no. I wasn't suggesting him."

"Then who?"

"I don't know. I don't know. Can't you see I'm upset? How would you feel if someone you had trusted had done something like this right under your nose?"

"Who, Effield? You? Someone put those fake new addresses in the case folders."

He stared directly at me. "What kind of woman are you? Don't you have any feelings? I told you I'm upset."

"You're upset! Think about what happened to Anne Spaulding!"

Effield's eyes dropped. "I've told you what I know; I've even made guesses about things I don't know. What more do you want?"

There might have been something else to squeeze out

of him, but I doubted it, and time was what I did not have. Warning Effield not to touch Anne's cases, I started out of his office. Anyone here could have known. Anyone. Nat included.

Chapter

Fern was gone. Nat was gone. But Mona, who had been packing up twenty minutes ago, was leaning back in her chair, swivelled to face Effield's office door, waiting. She smiled at me.

I smiled back. We had here a meeting of the minds. My only question was where to go to talk privately, but that was answered by the banging of the back door and the sight of Alec Effield making his way to the street.

I sat in Fern's chair. "What do you know about dummy cases, Mona?"

"Theoretically, or in fact?"

"In fact, Mona. Here in the office."

Her eyes opened wide. "Really? Anne? Wow!"

"You suspected it?"

"Not specifically. I mean, I didn't know if Anne was up to something, but I'm not surprised. How'd she do it?"

"You tell me. How would the money go out and get back to Anne?"

Mona glanced around, scanning the empty chairs. Above her desk, a clock ticked against the silence of the room. "I can't swear to you how Anne did it, but here's the way it would logically work," she said. "Setting up a dummy would be no problem. Once the case is ready the money goes out via computer check to the address. Then it's just a matter of picking it up and getting false I.D.'s to cash the checks. Anyone with half a mind can get phony cards. It's been written up in magazines, and most of the news shows on television have shown it step by step. You could cash the checks at the supermarket. After all, the checks are good." Mona paused. "The only thing is, Anne's left-handed. And her handwriting is distinctly awful. All the phony signatures must look alike."

I recalled that crabbed writing I had had to get Pereira to decipher. "She could have varied it."

"No. I saw her try once. She needed to sign Fern's name to an emergency action—to get a food order for a client—and even with Fern's signature there to copy she couldn't do it."

And Anne had been unable to draw the simple sketch for the *Rhinoceros* handbill. Still, I said, "Maybe it was for your benefit."

Mona snorted. "I'd have known."

"Maybe. Certainly you're pretty clear on how to create dummies."

"Jesus! You don't suspect me!" She looked truly outraged.

"You know how to set up the dummies," I repeated. "And, Mona, you were at Bank of America, hanging around on the first of two consecutive months."

"I told you, I was thinking of opening an account."

"That's what you *told* me."

"Well, I don't have an account. I . . ."

"Could we skip to the truth?"

When she didn't answer, I said, "First you're at Alec's flat. Then you make a point of riding down the hill with me and asking questions about Anne. Then you invite me over to confer. You're awfully interested in this case. Could it be that you were part of the dummy case racket?

Did you kill Anne when she tried to cheat you?" I took a breath. "What were you doing at the bank, Mona?"

Mona stared, amazed.

"I found a long brown curly hair in one of the dummy case files—a hair like yours. Nat overheard you arguing with Alec and Anne. What—"

"Okay. Okay. I was at the bank." With a sigh, she leaned back in the chair. "I *had* gone in to get some information on accounts, savings accounts. That was the truth."

"And?"

"Well, the bank was jammed. It was the first of the month. Every welfare client was in there cashing a check. I'd forgotten it was the first, or I'd never have gone in there. Anyway, I was trying to decide if it was worth it to see a bank officer when I noticed Alec standing to one side of the tellers. That's where you sign to get into a safe-deposit box. Of course, I didn't know that then. I started over to ask him if he had any idea how long I'd have to wait, since he was obviously familiar with the bank. His side was to me, and as I came toward him he turned away to face the teller. I heard Alec give a name to the teller, and the teller repeat it. Then Alec followed the teller inside."

I waited.

"The name, you see, it wasn't Alec Effield."

"What was it?"

"Johnson."

"Johnson? Do you know the first name?"

"No." She looked put out.

"Mona, Johnson is one of the most common names in the country, almost as common as Smith."

Mona forced a smile. "Maybe that's why he chose it."

"Then what happened?"

"What do you mean?"

"At the bank, Mona. What happened?"

"Nothing. Nothing happened. I left."

"Okay," I said. It wasn't okay at all, but I continued.

"That was the first time you were there. What about the next month?"

"Someone saw me both times?"

"Uh huh. What did you do the second time?"

"Nothing." Seeing my growing anger, she added quickly, "I just waited from twelve to one. But Alec didn't come. Maybe he came later. Or maybe not."

I stared at Mona, picturing her not in her violet T-shirt and peasant skirt, not with her loose breasts straining the fabric, but with the right make-up and a wig, with a brassiere and a blazer. Mona transformed.

"Listen, I could have found out about Alec. I still could. He's easy to play; he'll tell me."

I stood up. "As soon as I leave here I'm going to call in and have someone keep an eye on you. Don't try to leave Berkeley without checking with me."

I didn't call in for a tail. For the moment my bluff would keep Mona here.

Instead I drove across the crowded Friday evening streets, pulling from lane to lane, running yellow lights. My foot pressed harder on the gas pedal as I recalled Alec Effield spurting crocodile tears and telling me how worried he was about his reputation.

Leaving my car behind Effield's, I ran toward his flat, up the stairs and banged on the door.

Inside it was dark. There was no music. I glanced at my watch—six-fifteen. I banged again.

"Open up, Effield."

A light came on in the main house. A face peered out from behind a shade. No sound came from Effield's. Effield might be out. He could be dining at some expensive French restaurant, on the money from those dummy cases.

I pounded once more, but the realization was coming clear: Effield might be inside, hiding, and there was nothing I could do. I had no actual proof that he was Anne's accomplice. There was only Mona's word that he was in the bank. And as I'd thought while staring at her, "Johnson" could be, not Alec Effield, but Mona.

Alec Effield could be merely a dupe.

Chapter

"Alec Effield could be a dupe." I was standing against the sink, as Howard pulled the leftover lasagna from his fridge. In the living room a guy in a 49ers shirt was watching a Japanese horror movie. Upstairs, lights and music blared from the six bedrooms of the old house. A woman clad in only bikini pants ran across the landing. I hadn't seen the inside of a place like this since college.

Howard had been to my apartment and never raised an eyebrow. Now I could understand why.

Howard and I had been friends, close friends, for three years. In a sense it was strange I'd never been here before. But it was no accident. When I'd been married to Nat, visiting Howard would have created more discord than there already was. Most of the time, there had been arguments and bad feelings enough. And I had kept my distance for other reasons. Howard was my friend, but there was more to it than that, and I hadn't wanted to explore that area then. And after the divorce, I hadn't wanted to explore anything. Mostly I'd wanted to be left alone. And now? I didn't know exactly.

"You mind eating cold lasagna?" Howard asked.

"What?"

"There's something wrong with the oven. Do you mind eating the lasagna cold?"

I laughed. "A little touch of home. No, cold's fine with me. But listen, about Alec Effield, if he is a dupe, then Anne's accomplice could be Mona."

"Wait, wait. Start from the beginning. When I last caught this saga we were leaving Priester's and you had come up with something that you promised to tell me later." Handing me the lasagna pan, he picked up two bottles of Coke and plates. The forks peeked out of his shirt pocket.

I followed him to the dining room table. Out of the side of my eye I could see terrified Japanese shouting in ill-dubbed English.

"Hey, Wayne," Howard called, "could you watch that in your room?"

I took a bite of lasagna. Even cold, it was good. "The beginning," I said, as Wayne trudged up the stairs. "Well, Anne Spaulding had two scams going. First she was taking bribes from clients on the Avenue, probably about twenty dollars a throw."

Howard took a swallow of Coke. "Pretty small time."

"My guess is that it was her first taste of crime. The dummy cases followed. Even Effield admitted Anne would have had no trouble working dummies."

"How would she have done it?"

"Easier than you'd think. She could pretend she had interviewed the clients, set up the cases, and have the checks sent out. Then it would be just a matter of picking them up."

"I assume she didn't do that herself, trotting from house to house, like the farmer's daughter collecting eggs."

"No. There was the black woman who has been seen picking up checks in the hotel lobby. The woman Daisy Arbutus saw."

Howard cut a bite of lasagna, forked it and held it in

readiness. "So you think the black woman picked up the money and then she or Spaulding forged the signatures and—"

"No."

"No? Then what?"

"Anne Spaulding couldn't copy anything. There's over-whelming agreement on that."

"Then the other woman signed them?"

Absently, I followed the passage of lasagna from fork into Howard's mouth. Normally his conclusion would have made sense, but from all I had heard of Anne Spaulding, I couldn't believe she would allow another woman so much power. "No. What would keep the black woman from walking off with the profits? It's not like Anne could report her."

Howard finished his Coke and held the bottle aloft to check for any last drops.

"According to Mona Liebowitz, Alec Effield was at the bank using an alias to get into a safe-deposit box."

He put down the bottle. "So, somehow the money got from the hotels to him and he put it in the safe-deposit box. Maybe keeping it in a safe-deposit box was insurance against any one of them betraying the others."

"How do you mean?"

"Well, for one thing it's much safer than keeping that amount of money at home, particularly when two fellow crooks know it's there. Obviously, none of them could put their gains in regular bank accounts, and there's only so much they could spend before they drew atten-tion to themselves."

"But what do you mean by insurance?"

"Okay. Suppose Anne and Alec sign for the box as Mr. and Mrs. Johnson. That means that only they have ac-cess to the box. Things balance out between them and the black woman; they have access to the accumulated loot; she has first access to each month's take. She could make off with the monthly money, but no more. While they control the ongoing take, they are still dependent on her each month. And . . ." With his right foot How-

ard nudged his empty plate over, then he propped both
feet where it had been.

"And?"

"And there's the key."

"Go on."

"The key to the safe-deposit box. The bank has one
key. The depositor has one or two keys. Obviously Alec
Effield has a key."

"I can see where that gives Alec control and the black
woman control. But it doesn't seem to insure Anne."

"Maybe Anne didn't need any more control than she
managed through force of personality."

"Possible. But Anne sounds like someone who would
leave no unnecessary escape hatch." I moved a piece of
my lasagna around on my plate. "Another possibility is
that Mona could be lying about the whole safe-deposit
thing, or any part, and she could be the accomplice."

"And the black woman?"

"Mona, with make-up, wig, other clothing."

"Would she pass?"

I realized Howard hadn't seen Mona. "It's not like
making a Swede into a pigmy. Weston, the guy at the
wheelchair theater, was telling me how much make-up
can do. And with Mona it would be no problem at all."

"So then you're saying that Anne Spaulding set up the
dummies and Mona collected the money, signed the
checks, and put the cash in the safe-deposit box."

"I'm saying maybe. Maybe Alec Effield was in the
bank. Maybe he signed the checks. He's good at copying,
Howard. Very good." I told him about the Suzanne
Valadon copy in Effield's office. "He even told me copying wasn't valuable outside the criminal world."

Things were falling into place. "The new addresses on
the memos in Anne's cases," I said. "Effield wrote them
after he killed Anne. He had access to the cases. They
were in his office."

"Or Mona Liebowitz could have gotten to them. It
doesn't sound like a tightly run office. But . . ." Howard
took a bite of my barely touched lasagna. "But, sticking

with Effield for the moment, if he's involved, then who is the black woman?"

"I don't know. I'll have to find Effield."

The streets were dark now as I drove the familiar route across town to Alec Effield's place. Why couldn't he be home when I needed him, or at least live closer?

It was nearly ten-thirty. Cars struggled along the main thoroughfares, cars filled with people coming home from movies, or going for a drink. No one was in a hurry. No one was making way for anyone else in a hurry. I was tempted to use the pulser, but we'd all been cautioned about resorting to it too freely.

I turned onto Spruce, winding higher up into the hills. Here two-hundred-thousand-dollar houses sat on their narrow lots like fans in the bleachers. Their lights were muted by the fog. I pulled into Effield's street and stopped the car behind his.

Effield's flat was still dark. I stomped up the stairs, prepared to bang long and hard on the door.

The door stood ajar. I pushed it and walked in, calling Effield's name and feeling around on the wall for the light switch.

"Ef—" I stopped, swallowing a scream. It was a moment before I could force myself to look again.

Effield lay sprawled across the beige couch, his head hanging over the back, his eyes locked open in terror. Blood, dark red, nearly brown, stained his red shirt. It had run onto his beige pants. It had splattered on the beige couch and on the beige rug.

There was no need to feel for Effield's pulse. It didn't take a doctor to see that his throat had been cut, the carotid artery severed. His blood had pumped out like water from a garden hose.

Steeling myself, refusing to succumb to the nausea rising in my stomach, I turned away from Effield's body and surveyed the room. There was no sound, and few hiding places. Taking out my automatic, I pulled open the closet door. It held only clothes. I checked the other rooms, but the killer had gone.

Then I called the station. The beat officer would be notified. The lab crew would arrive. The coroner would come. Another officer would take Mona Liebowitz to the station.

The weapon didn't require much searching. Effield's brass letter opener lay behind the sofa, the blood still on the blade and, from a cursory glance, I figured the hilt had been wiped clean. Only a thin streak of blood remained.

The beat officer came through the door at the same time as the back-up crew. After he surveyed the scene and shook off the sight of Effield's body, I told him about the case.

Then came the search of the flat, and the ground—painstaking, inch-by-inch work, circumscribed by the beams of flashlights. It hadn't rained in months; there would be no footprints.

The ground showed nothing. The flat was a zero, unless some of the fingerprints turned out to be useful. But I doubted that. The killer had been careful enough to wipe the knife. And besides, everyone in Effield's unit had been here for the party Monday night. Fingerprints would prove nothing.

But the safe-deposit key, which I expected to find on Effield's key ring or in a drawer, was definitely not in the flat. Either the killer had taken it, or Effield had had it only long enough to get into the box. I suspected the latter—that there was only one key. Even split three ways it was too much money to spend without attracting attention, or to keep at home safely. So the black woman collected the checks from the hotels, Effield signed them, and Anne, the black woman, or both cashed them. Then Anne or Effield put the money in the safe-deposit box and gave the key to the black woman. Anne and Effield had the signatures; the black woman had the key. A good, safe arrangement. Then neither Effield nor Anne nor the black woman would be able to take the money alone.

It was four A.M. when I closed up the house. When I'd driven here I had expected Alec Effield to tell me who the black woman was. I had felt sure I could get him to talk.

Doubtless she, too, realized how close he was to breaking, and having killed once . . . With Effield dead the secret of her identity was safe.

Or was it? I did, after all, have a witness who had seen her.

Chapter

25

Quentin Delehanty was lying on his side, snoring like a recording from Sri Fallon's.

I stepped into his cell and shook him. "Get up, Delehanty."

He gurgled, turned, eyes still closed, and began to snore louder.

I shook him again, and kept shaking till his eyes opened.

It was a couple of minutes before he realized where he was and why. And it wasn't till he had walked from the cell to the interviewing area and consumed two cups of machine coffee that he was clearheaded enough to talk. Even then he didn't look crisp, but whatever lucidity he could muster I considered a boon.

"Are you with me, Mr. Delehanty?" I asked.

He nodded, slowly; each head-raising motion seemed an effort.

"Okay." I waited till he looked up. "Who was the black woman with you at Anne Spaulding's house Monday night?"

"Huh?"

"Anne Spaulding's."

His head hung. I wondered if he hadn't heard or if he was just playing for time.

"Delehanty, answer the question."

"I need more coffee."

"After you answer."

He shrugged, a small movement. It tired him. "Yes, I was there."

I motioned the clerk for more coffee. "Bring a couple." To Delehanty, I said, "You were there when she was killed. What happened?"

The coffee cup shook in his hand. "What? Killed? Is she dead?"

"Look, Delehanty, you were there, one of the last persons there. There's blood all over the room. You left, got drunk, and stayed drunk until we brought you in here. Are you trying to tell me nothing happened at Anne Spaulding's?"

The clerk put down the fresh coffees. Delehanty gulped one. He gasped at the heat, but the shock seemed to wake him. He looked at me. "Let me tell you what happened. I do remember. I have a very good memory. Surprising for one of my habits, isn't it? But I haven't always been a drunk. I used to hold quite a respectable job."

"What about Monday night?"

He winced. "Of course. Well, as background, let me tell you that Anne Spaulding enjoyed cheating people. She was completely dishonest. She—" He stopped as he noticed my expression. I didn't have time for another account of Anne Spaulding's character.

Shifting in his chair, Delehanty said, "Last week, that bitch cut off Tad Yeville."

"Your friend who overdosed?"

"Yeah. When I heard, I was furious. I'm still furious. Look at my hands, they're shaking. I started to drink, then I thought, no, that bitch won't get away with it. I knew where her place was. I'd seen her when I went to

Sri Fallon's. I went there. I told her about Tad. Do you think she cared, even then? Do you?" He glared at me.

"Did she?"

"Not shit. But she was scared. I told her this was the end. I was going to make her pay. I was going to the papers, the police, Legal Aid, and whoever else would listen. I was going to tell them about her shaking down clients on the Avenue. That would be it. Jail."

"And?"

"She laughed. Real cool. She said no one would believe me. Maybe she was right, I don't know, but it made me so mad that I picked up a lamp and came at her."

I held my breath.

"I raised the lamp. It hit the door. The edges were jagged. I smashed it at her—her arms and her shoulders. She was scared. She caught my arm. God, she was strong. She pulled the lamp out of my hand. She came at me with it." He flung open his shirt. "Look."

There were scabs on his shoulders, upper chest and arms. He could have bled a lot from those.

"Then what happened?"

"I started for her, but she hit me again. God, she was strong. She got cut up too, like I said, on her upper arms and her shoulders. Do you want to see the bruises on my legs?"

I shook my head, recalling the blood-spotted linen dress. The blood was on the sleeves and the bodice. Delehanty's explanation fit.

"Well, the whole thing really put me off balance. She slammed the bedroom door and I just stood there, pressing on the wounds to stop the bleeding. I must have stood there for ten minutes. I was going to pound on the bedroom door again, but somehow it didn't seem important. I just picked up my windbreaker and walked out."

"Anne was still alive?" I asked.

"Sure."

"You walked out?"

"I stood on the porch, letting the cool air bring me around. I decided to go back. I started to bang on the

door and changed my mind. Then I went upstairs to Sri
Fallon's."

"Didn't he notice the blood?"

Delehanty shook his head. "No. My hands were okay.
My windbreaker covered the cuts. Anyway, I didn't stay.
I was too hopped up. I couldn't get into it. I left."

"After how long?"

"Ten minutes, maybe."

I wrote quickly, letting Delehanty start on another cup
of coffee. I could imagine Anne Spaulding's panic. Once
an investigation started it wouldn't be long before it
moved from her shaking down street artists to exploring
whatever she was up to with those hotel cases. Delehanty
had been threatening to expose more than he realized.

It all fit in. Anne was scared but alive when he left her
with the black woman. Pencil poised, I asked, "The black
woman, Delehanty, who was she?"

Delehanty looked up, his bushy gray eyebrows trying
to arch in surprise. "What black woman?"

"The one at Anne Spaulding's."

He put down the coffee cup. "Come on, Officer, I was
straight with you. Don't be like that."

"Delehanty, who was she?"

"Officer, there was no one there but me and Spaulding.
We were screaming and fighting. You think someone else
was there just watching?"

"I didn't say just watching."

He stared directly at me and spoke slowly. "There was
no one there but me and Spaulding. No one, black or
white."

"Look, Delehanty," I said, straining to keep a sem-
blance of calm, "we've got a lot against you—resisting
arrest, drunk and disorderly, inciting a mob—don't press
your luck."

"There was no one there. What do I have to tell you?"

"A witness saw a black woman."

He drew in his breath, lifted the empty cup and put it
down again. "I wish there had been a black woman
there, then you'd be coming down on her instead of me.

I hate Spaulding. If she's dead, I won't be going to her funeral. But I am civilized. I don't condone murder, and I damn well don't put myself between the murderer and the police. So believe me, if I knew of anyone, I'd be jumping up to tell you."

"I'll get some more coffee." I wanted the time to think. Delehanty seemed straight. Had the black woman been hiding in the house? Had he seen her but forgotten? Or had she indeed not been there at all? I hurried with the coffee. If I took time to sift the information through, Delehanty would go back to sleep.

Putting the cups before him, I said, "To save us both time, I'm going to tell you that I know your hotel is used as a mail drop. I know people hang around the lobby on the first of the month waiting for checks to be delivered. One of them was a black woman."

Delehanty thought a minute, then nodded.

"What did she look like?"

He shrugged. "She was a black woman with an Afro."

"Tall, short, light, or dark?"

"I don't remember."

"Come on."

"No, honestly. I remember the Afro. It was big. I guess she couldn't have been too big, because the size of the Afro really stood out."

"What about her color?"

He appeared to be trying to remember. He shook his head. "I only recall seeing her from the back."

"Was she Ermentine Brown?"

Delehanty shrugged. "I know Ermentine, but I wouldn't recognize her from the back."

"What about Yvonne McIvor?"

"Who?"

"Yvonne McIvor."

"Don't know her."

"She lived in the hotel."

"Wouldn't be her, then. There's no reason to hang around the lobby if you live there. The walls are so thin you can hear everything from your room. And when the mailman gets there on the first there's plenty to hear."

"Well, then, who was she?"

Delehanty slammed down his hand, spilling the remaining coffee. "I told you, I don't know. It could have been anyone."

But it couldn't have been *anyone*.

If Alec Effield had been in the bank, as Mona told me, then the accomplice was an unknown black woman. If I could prove Alec had not been in the bank, if Alec were not the safe-deposit box Johnson, then the accomplice was Mona.

And that, Sri Fallon would remember.

Chapter

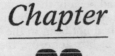

Everything looked the same as it had the first day I'd come to Sri Fallon's building. Curtains were drawn in both apartments—Anne's just as I had left them.

A low moan snaked down from the upstairs flat. I tried the door, was not surprised to find it open, and made my way up the dark purple stairway into the incense-heavy room.

Fallon sat at the far end, back to me, facing a small altar. Between us ten devotees sat cross-legged, eyes closed. All chanted softly, in fear, I supposed, of the neighbors.

Stepping around the devotees, I made my way to Fallon, tapped his shoulder and when his eyes remained closed, hissed, "I have to talk to you, now."

His eyes opened slowly, his mouth pulled down in irritation before he controlled his face and the calm expression returned. Nodding, he bowed to the altar and motioned me toward the back, into the kitchen.

"I'm sorry to disturb you. . . ."

He nodded, cutting me off.

"Do you remember the woman you saw in the welfare office the other day?"

He nodded again.

"She was in the bank—"

Another nod.

"Does she have an account there?"

He shook his head.

"A safe-deposit box?"

"No."

I could barely hear his whisper. "Would it be easier to talk outside?" I asked.

He opened the door and led me out onto a wooden landing from which stairs led down to the ground. For a group that chanted as loud as this one, they took great precautions to protect themselves from disturbance.

I pulled out a picture of Alec Effield I had gotten from the beat officer. "Have you seen this man at the bank?"

He stared at it. "Yes."

"Does *he* have an account?"

"I don't think so."

"Safe-deposit box?"

"Yes, that's it."

"Do you remember his name?"

Sri Fallon closed his eyes.

I waited then asked, "Was it Effield?"

"No, no. That doesn't sound right."

"Johnson?"

"Perhaps. It doesn't ring a bell, but a common name like that wouldn't."

"Was the woman in the welfare office with him?"

He thought a moment, then said, "No."

"Was there a woman with him at all?"

"No."

"Thanks."

I made my way back through the chanters. It was just six A.M. as I stepped outside. The chanting was now audible on the street, and I found to my surprise it was not so irritating as I had at first thought. Of course, I was awake, and it was just a matter of time till I brought in a murderer.

I drove quickly. The streets were still empty. I knew I should feel tired, but I didn't. A day ago I was tired. Now I was exhilarated.

Double-parking in front of the station I ran in.

Mona Liebowitz was sitting downstairs under the eye of one of the rookies. Her feet were drawn up under her, a tired and very angry expression marked her face. When she saw me, her frown deepened. "I've been here half the night—"

"I had to check your story, about Effield in the bank. It checks. You'll be able to go home soon."

"Does that mean you know who killed Alec?"

"I just need to be sure of one thing. You can tell me." Mona sat up, feet on the floor. "Sure."

Once again, the case hinged on those dummy folders. I thought of them as I first had seen them in Anne's office —the manila folders had held four or five legal-size forms, no small memos with address changes, no notes, no NCR copies. "Mona," I said, "what do you put on receipts when you give them to clients?"

"What receipts?"

"The ones you give clients for the verifications you take from them. What do you give a client when you take her rent verification?"

Mona leaned forward. "I never give receipts. They're just more work."

"What did Anne do?"

"Anne? Well, she was a different story. Anne was nothing if not careful. She'd take an NCR pad—they're in all the booths—people are always walking off with them. Anne would write something simple, like such-and-such was received on such-and-such a date, and sign it."

"And the copy?"

"In the case folder."

"It was always in the case folder?"

"Anne always covered herself." Mona pressed her lips

together. "She always watched out for herself. She was not a trusting soul."

"Do you have a key to the office?"

"Sure. We all do."

"I need it."

I went straight to Effield's desk and opened the McIvor folder. The copy of the NCR note was on the right side. Taking it out I held it and the original Yvonne McIvor had given me up to the light. It was the copy, all right. No forgery, this.

I also knew the receipt had not been in the case folder the last time I looked through it. It had been put there after Effield had shown the folder to me at four-thirty yesterday afternoon.

Leaning against the desk, I pictured Yvonne as she had scurried around searching for the NCR note.

I realized how wrong I had been about the case. From the first, I had been wrong.

Chapter

27

I called the dispatcher for a back-up, not sure I would need one.

The shops below the apartment were dark; they wouldn't be open for hours. The stairway to the door seemed more tunnel-like than ever and I had to bang four times before I got even a groggy answer.

"Open up. It's the police."

"What?"

Inside the apartment I could hear feet scurrying, the thwack of things being bumped into. It was a good five minutes before the door opened, revealing Yvonne Mc-Ivor.

"It's the middle of the night. What do you want?"

"First, I want to come in."

She stepped back automatically and I pushed in before she had time to think.

"You're under arrest for embezzlement and for the murder of Alec Effield."

Her mouth dropped open. Her head moved back and

forth, trying to shake loose the sleepy hangover from the night. She was deciding her next move.

"Listen, lady," she said, forcing her face into a bewildered expression, "you've made a mistake. I'm just livin' here on the county, tryin' to get by."

"It's too late for that. It was a good act, a very good act, but you blew it with that receipt."

She edged away from me, but I kept between her and the door.

"Why did you kill Effield? Was I getting too close? Did you realize it was only a matter of time till I got proof of his involvement?"

She moved closer to the door, but it led only to the bedroom and bathroom.

"He would have talked, wouldn't he? He would have turned you in, after you'd arranged such a foolproof escape."

She was in front of the bedroom door, her hand on the frame.

"With Effield dead, all the money is yours, or it would have been if you could have waited till Monday and gotten to the safe-deposit box. Isn't that right, isn't—"

She jumped back into the bedroom and slammed the door.

I grabbed for the knob just as the lock clicked in place.

"Open up! You're just making it worse. There's nowhere to go!"

But there was somewhere to go. I rushed to the window in time to see her leap down to the roof of the next building.

Pushing open the living room window, I jumped after her, my feet hitting hard against the tar and gravel. She had fifty feet on me, racing across the rooftops, her long legs moving with ease under the loose dashiki. I remembered her bedroom. She was an athlete, probably in as good condition as I.

I cleared the wall onto the second-to-last building, my equipment belt banging heavily on my hipbones. She was on the last roof. I ran to it, clambering over the wall, just in time to see her lower herself over the far edge.

Racing across, I looked down—twelve feet—grabbed the roof and pushed off, coming down hard.

"Stop!" I yelled. But she was gone. Nothing moved; no door stood open; no dust floated up from the alley.

Behind me was the row of buildings we had just run across. The metal doors were shut. To my right was an open field. In front were houses, each with a fenced yard. She had to be in one of them—one of the closer ones; she'd had only a few seconds on me.

That narrowed the choice to four. Dismissing one with a see-through picket fence, and two with eight-foot hedges, I headed for the remaining one.

I boosted myself up till I could see over the six-foot fence. The yard was made for a fugitive. It held a tool shed, garbage cans, thick bushes. There was no sign of her, but that didn't mean she wasn't there. It was a chance I had to take.

I hoisted myself to the top and as I was coming over, a rock smashed into my hand. Blood flowed. I dropped to the ground.

She stood by the shed, a sharp, flat rock poised in her hand.

"Put it down!" I yelled.

She turned, hurling it like a shot put. I jumped to the side. The rock slashed my face.

I started for my gun, but stopped. There could be people by the windows in the house. A bullet could ricochet.

I moved in.

She grabbed a spade. "Come on, cop."

"Put it down!"

"Come on!"

Her bare legs were planted wide apart. Both hands were on the shovel, ready to swing. If I went for my gun now, she'd have the spade on my neck. Where was the back-up unit? Would they be able to find me when they arrived?

She moved toward me slowly. She was three feet away, judging her shot.

I stepped back.

She leaped forward, hoisting the spade. I grabbed the shovel end, the metal searing into my fingers. Lunging forward, I jammed the handle at her chest. She jumped away, dropping it. It banged into my leg.

She made for the gate. I grabbed her leg, pulled her to the ground. She rolled over, kicked into my stomach. I fell. She yanked my hair. My scream sounded distant.

Joining both hands, I smashed them down, but she rolled free and pushed herself to her knees. Gasping for breath, I turned and brought my left hand down hard on her neck.

She lay stunned.

I clambered up, grabbed my gun and held it over her.

She lay there, dashiki covered in dirt, her Afro wig lying against the wall, her own hair blond with dark roots.

I said, "Get up, Anne."

Chapter

28

"Yvonne McIvor was really Anne Spaulding?" Lt. Davis's forehead was lined in amazement.

The doctor had looked at my bruised face and the cuts and scrapes on my hands. I felt like a six-year-old. Lt. Davis had counted my overtime toward Watch and given me the rest of the day off. And Anne Spaulding was in a cell, refusing to talk, waiting for her lawyer. It was nearly eleven A.M.

"Yes. Anne had used the disguise to collect the checks from the dummy cases. That's why she had two different shades of make-up, why she had a sunlamp, why she sunbathed only one week a month."

"Smith." He shook his head again. "I just can't believe a white woman could impersonate a black all that easily."

I suppressed a grin at the lieutenant's bruised racial pride. "It wasn't easy. It was very careful and well-planned. Spaulding's one outside interest was the theater. She wasn't doing this part cold. She had all the accoutrements—the wig, the dashiki, and a lot of experience with make-up. She's seen plenty of black women in the welfare office, enough to pick up speech patterns, to observe gestures and movements."

"Still, another black would know."

"Maybe, Lieutenant, but Spaulding in the person of Yvonne McIvor didn't come into contact with other blacks. She walked into hotels, waited silently and walked out. Probably the only time she had to talk was when she cashed checks, opened bank accounts, or when she signed for the safe-deposit box. There are enough white people around so she would never have to deal with a black."

"Maybe."

"It worked, Lieutenant. If someone had pressed her she could always be rude, tell them to fuck off. When that happens the first question that comes to your mind isn't, 'Is this person really black?'"

"Yeah, okay." He fingered my report. "Give me your reasoning."

I settled back. The Morning Watch commander had let us use the office. It was relatively tidy, only a few papers spread around, but Lt. Davis pushed at the edges, and I knew if it had been his shift, everything would have been in squared-off piles. "When Delehanty threatened to report her for taking bribes, Anne Spaulding realized that the dummy case racket would also be exposed. She couldn't be sure Delehanty hadn't told someone already. The safest way out was to have Anne Spaulding disappear. Fortunately, she had plenty of identities to melt into."

"And she chose McIvor?"

"No. Initially she just lit out of the apartment, leaving her purse and all her belongings, which she wouldn't be able to use anyway, and she contacted Effield, her partner. Then, when I demanded to see one of the dummy cases, Effield let me choose one. Whatever name I chose, Anne took."

"But how did she get the McIvor apartment?"

"I can't be sure till we check with the landlord, but

probably Anne and Alec had rented it when they started the dummy case scheme and Anne used it as a place to go in the McIvor disguise, after she'd collected the checks. It was perfect for that—cheap and secluded."

Lt. Davis fingered his moustache. "Then Effield was responsible for leaving Spaulding's clothing by the Bay?"

"He had to get rid of the clothes, and doing it that way he could give the impression her body had been thrown in the Bay." I paused, reordering my thoughts. Taking a breath, I said, "When I was at the McIvor apartment, I looked into the bedroom, which, incidentally, was in the same state of disorder as Anne's own apartment. Mixed in with her black trappings, she had a ski-wear magazine. Welfare clients don't have ski-wear magazines. They don't consider what will be fashionable on the slopes; they worry about where next month's rent is coming from."

The lieutenant nodded.

"But the real tip-off was the NCR note acknowledging Yvonne's rent receipt. Welfare clients carry all their important papers in their purses, because they may need them at the welfare office. It's like a briefcase to a lawyer. If Yvonne really had been a client, she would have had the NCR note in her purse Thursday. She would have looked there first. But there wasn't any NCR note. She took her purse into the bathroom to write one in, of course, Anne Spaulding's own handwriting. Then, always careful to cover herself, she had Effield put the copy in the case folder. But I had checked the folder before—there was no NCR copy in it."

"Yet and still," the lieutenant said, "it seems like Anne Spaulding put a lot of trust in Effield. What was to keep him from leaving with the money any time?"

Anne Spaulding had said nothing, but I'd given this question some thought. "For one thing, there was Anne's personality and Alec's. No question who was the strong one. Alec must have known Anne wouldn't let him get away with that. I suspect when we get the court order and open that box we'll find virtually the whole amount of money still there."

The lieutenant said nothing.

"We went over Effield's flat very carefully. There was no safe-deposit key. We found it in the McIvor apartment. That was Anne's insurance. I doubt Effield saw that key any time but the day he made his deposit. So Anne had the key and Alec had the signature. Neither one could get the money without the other."

The lieutenant smiled. He'd been up since he got the word on Effield. Nothing happened to one of his officers without his knowing. But he didn't look tired. He was running on success. "Good job, Smith."

"Thanks." I pushed myself up. The elation I had experienced a few hours ago had worn off. The image of Alec Effield's body remained. I walked toward my desk, ready to assemble my notes and dictate the report before going home.

The case was over—almost. One loose end remained. Nat.

I was exhausted, but at the same time wired. If I went home I wouldn't sleep. If I sat in the sun, I'd think about dealing with Nat. Neither of us would be at his best now, but that wouldn't matter.

Nat looked spent as he opened the door of his house. His hair hung uncombed from his center part, his skin was gray and sagged into the hollows of his cheeks. He looked like he was running on caffeine alone.

All my anger evaporated. I could berate him, as he well deserved, but there'd be no satisfaction from that. Watching him walk into the living room and sink onto the sofa, I felt a rush of the old tenderness, the protectiveness I'd felt at those rare moments when he'd revealed to me some fear or sense of desolation he could uncover in front of no one else. I wanted to hold him to me and to make it all right.

But I could change nothing. And reviving that very

unrepresentative aspect of our past would help neither of us. I sat on the chair opposite him.

"Do you know about Anne?"

"Yes."

"The dummy cases? Picking up the checks from the hotels?"

"Yes."

"And that she killed Alec Effield?"

"Yes." His voice was as gray as his face.

"Nat, you owe me an explanation of . . . of what you didn't tell me."

"Not now." He didn't look up. His voice was barely audible. It was almost as if, to him, I weren't even there.

"Now," I said.

"Jill, I'm too stunned to deal with all that."

My tenderness was gone. "Nat, I realize this is a bad time for you. It's not great for me. Twelve hours ago I found Alec Effield's corpse, with his throat cut. I've been up all night. I've been in a fight. But I started this investigation as a favor to you. Now I'm calling in that favor."

Nat hesitated.

I waited.

"Okay."

"Tell me what really happened with Anne, with your pen, and why you called me to begin with."

"I . . ." He stared down at his knees. "I don't know. I thought I knew. I thought Anne was so special. She was so interested in literature, in Yeats, in my thesis. We were so close: two kindred souls mired in the absurdity of the welfare department. Or so I thought. Apparently I was wrong, totally wrong, totally deceived, used. It never occurred to me that Anne could be a thief. I couldn't have imagined it."

"Did you think she was more honest?"

"I . . . it's not that." He pushed the hair back out of his face and said slowly, "I thought she had pierced through the bourgeois etiquette of life. I thought she was beyond that." He paused, looking away. "But she wasn't."

I could have reminded him she had fooled many others. But I said nothing. This was something he'd have to deal with alone.

I wanted to ask him what exactly his relationship was with Anne. Just close friends? Or were they lovers? But I caught myself. I didn't need to know for the case. And for myself, suddenly it didn't much matter. Instead, I said, "Why weren't you honest about your pewter pen?"

"I couldn't be, Jill. One night when I was at Anne's apartment, she asked to borrow it. She was taken with it, with its design. It was nice to be able to give her something of mine she admired. But I couldn't have told you that. If I'd even admitted that I gave it to her, you would have suspected what that meant, and I would have had to explain my whole relationship with Anne. I called you on the spur of the moment. I was afraid something had happened to her. People are hurt, in accidents, attacked by psychos. If Anne had been in the hospital, no one would have called me. I would have had no way of knowing, you see."

I nodded.

"But then, by the time you asked me about the pen, it was clear Anne had not just been in an accident, that something more was going on, and that I really didn't know Anne at all. I . . . well, I just couldn't deal with telling that to you."

"And so you let me go on investigating in the dark, wasting days, endangering my whole career because I trusted you!"

"I didn't think. . . ."

"And you . . . never mind." I was going to tell him that his silence may well have given Anne enough time to kill Alec Effield. But there was no point. He'd think of that soon enough.

I was tempted to ask him what he would do now, if he would stay on at the welfare department. But I didn't.

I stood up. "Goodbye, Nat."

The scene with Nat must have drained what energy I had left. It had been only two in the afternoon when I got home, but I'd crawled into my sleeping bag. I had slept through whichever of the numerous pieces of electrical equipment Mr. Keppel had chosen to attack his lawn that Saturday afternoon; I'd slept through the evening and all night and had barely pulled open eyelids that seemed cemented shut when I heard a knock on the door.

"Who's there?"

"Howard."

"Howard?" I checked my watch. It was nearly ten A.M. I wriggled out of the bag, pulled on my robe and ran my fingers through my hair as I walked to the door.

"Did I get you up?" he asked, grinning down at me.

I laughed. "I can see I'm not likely to get much sympathy from you. It's nothing urgent, is it?" Howard had never just dropped in before.

"No. I can wait while you take a shower or whatever. I'll make us some coffee. If I remember your kitchen, it'll take me that long to find your Melitta."

"Okay." I headed for the shower and turned the water on hard. It was surprisingly comfortable having Howard here in the morning. I would like to have greeted him looking better, with combed hair, with enough make-up on to separate me from the dead. But Howard didn't seem to mind. It made a nice contrast to Nat. All those years Nat had had Anne's pedestal in reserve, waiting for someone worthy—not me—to grace it. It was nice not to be found wanting, indeed to be desirable. It was nice to have Howard making coffee.

Clean, make-up on, hair combed, I emerged from the bathroom twenty minutes later.

Howard was stretched out on the lounge chair.

"Where's that coffee you promised?" I asked.

"I tried. I searched through all the places any reasonable person would keep a Melitta, but there was no sign of it, to say nothing of papers or coffee."

"Oh."

"No big deal. I came to take you out to breakfast. Solv-

ing that case is going to look very good on your record.
It's a definite cause for celebration."

"Okay, thanks."

"Wear a dress."

"A dress? Are we going someplace special?"

"Priester's."

"Priester's has never had a dress code before."

Howard grinned. "Actually, this is a two-fold breakfast
—your celebration and a favor you can do for me."

"Yes?"

"You can sit next to me in Priester's, very cozily, and,
with luck, dash the hopes of Daisy Arbutus."

Match wits with the bestselling
MYSTERY WRITERS
in the business!

SARA PARETSKY
"Paretsky's name always makes the top of the list when people talk about the new female operatives." —*The New York Times Book Review*

☐ BLOOD SHOT	20420-8	$6.99
☐ BURN MARKS	20845-9	$6.99
☐ INDEMNITY ONLY	21069-0	$6.99
☐ GUARDIAN ANGEL	21399-1	$6.99
☐ KILLING ORDERS	21528-5	$6.99
☐ DEADLOCK	21332-0	$6.99
☐ TUNNEL VISION	21752-0	$6.99
☐ WINDY CITY BLUES	21873-X	$6.99
☐ A WOMAN'S EYE	21335-5	$6.99
☐ WOMEN ON THE CASE	22325-3	$6.99

HARLAN COBEN
Winner of the Edgar, the Anthony, and the Shamus Awards

☐ DEAL BREAKER	22044-0	$5.50
☐ DROP SHOT	22049-5	$5.50
☐ FADE AWAY	22268-0	$5.50
☐ BACK SPIN	22270-2	$5.50

RUTH RENDELL
"There is no finer mystery writer than Ruth Rendell." —*San Diego Union Tribune*

☐ THE CROCODILE BIND	21865-9	$5.99
☐ SIMISOLA	22202-8	$5.99
☐ KEYS TO THE STREET	22392-X	$5.99

LINDA BARNES

☐ COYOTE	21089-5	$5.99
☐ STEEL GUITAR	21268-5	$5.99
☐ BITTER FINISH	21606-0	$4.99
☐ SNAPSHOT	21220-0	$5.99
☐ CITIES OF THE DEAD	22095-5	$5.50
☐ DEAD HEAT	21862-4	$5.50
☐ HARDWARE	21223-5	$5.99

At your local bookstore or use this handy page for ordering:
DELL READERS SERVICE, DEPT. DIS
2451 South Wolf Road, Des Plaines, IL . 60018
Please send me the above title(s). I am enclosing $_____
(Please add $2.50 per order to cover shipping and handling.) Send check or money order—no cash or C.O.D.s please.

Dell

Ms./Mrs./Mr. _____

Address _____

City/State _____ Zip _____

DGM-12/97

Prices and availability subject to change without notice. Please allow four to six weeks for delivery.